CHRISTINA LAUREN

GALLERY BOOKS

NEW YORK • LONDON • TORONTO • SYDNEY • NEW DELHI

G

Gallery Books
An Imprint of Simon & Schuster, Inc.
1230 Avenue of the Americas
New York, NY 10020

This Gallery Books trade paperback edition March 2016

GALLERY BOOKS and colophon are registered trademarks
of Simon & Schuster, Inc.

For information about special discounts for bulk purchases,
please contact Simon & Schuster Special Sales at 1-866-506-1949
or business@simonandschuster.com.

The Simon & Schuster Speakers Bureau can bring authors
to your live event. For more information or to book an event,
contact the Simon & Schuster Speakers Bureau at 1-866-248-3049
or visit our website at www.simonspeakers.com.

Manufactured in the United States of America

10 9 8 7 6 5 4 3 2 1

Library of Congress Cataloging-in-Publication Data is available.

ISBN 978-1-5011-4622-0
ISBN 978-1-5011-3122-6 (ebook)

Beautiful
BOSS

ONE

Will

One drive to Boston down.

One rehearsal, one rehearsal *dinner*, one raucous night out with the guys down.

A wedding tomorrow, and one wife-to-be sleeping . . . down the hall.

I had a feeling this arrangement wouldn't last. Hanna hated sleeping apart on her recent trips for faculty position interviews nearly as much as I did. And the night before our wedding her mother gets us separate rooms, to *keep tradition, build suspense?*

Forget it.

It wouldn't last.

I reached behind me, fluffing the pillows, and then stretched out on the giant king-size bed.

My cell phone buzzed on the bedside table and I laughed, saying, "Called it," to the empty room before answering, "Hanna, my love."

She skipped the greeting entirely. "I'm nervous."

I smiled into the phone. "I'm not surprised. You're promising to obey me and be my sex slave for the remainder of your days. You know I won't go easy on you."

She didn't even spare me a laugh. "Can I come to your room?"

"Of course," I said. "I've been hoping you would come down—"

"*No*," she interrupted with force. "No, I can't. That was a *test*, Will. You're supposed to say it's bad luck."

"But I'm an atheist," I reminded her. "I don't believe in luck. I believe in intent. I believe in discovery. I believe in sex before the wedding. In fact, I believe you are three doors down, completely wigging out, when you could come in here and talk. And then let me put my penis in you. I'll stare at you the entire time, too, and our marriage will still be the most amazing marriage in the—"

"My boobs look enormous in my wedding dress."

I groaned, throwing my arm over my face. "Are you trying to kill me?"

"I just wanted to warn you." Her voice grew slightly slurred and I could immediately imagine her nervously chewing on a fingernail. "I think maybe it's overboard. I wanted it to be a cute thing between us—your boob obsession, our wedding; I mean, you—"

"Hanna," I cut in. "I promise to do my best not to motorboat you at the altar."

"That isn't what I mean."

"Plum. *Breathe*." I heard her take a long inhale and slowly let it out. "Tell me," I said quietly. "What *did* you mean?"

"Just that . . . what if I look . . ."

"Perfect?" I suggested.

She blew out a burst of air and admitted in a rush, "*Busty*—like a busty whore bride."

I held back a laugh, because while this was ridiculous to me, I knew it wasn't to her. "Are we seriously doing this right now? *This* is your pre-wedding freak-out? That your boobs will look too awesome tomorrow?"

Hanna had dealt with the wedding planning with ease, handing over the final details to her mom while she traveled all over for job interviews. She was being recruited by schools in nearly every corner of the country, sometimes going to two different places in a single week. And she'd never once complained about the madness of the past few months. I knew my Hanna was laid-back, but—*Jesus*—given everything, I had expected . . . *something*. A meltdown while we packed, maybe? But no, we got into a playful laundry war and ended up having sex in the hallway. Maybe a nitpicky fight on the drive up to Beantown? But no, she gave me head. Even a tantrum once we reached the hotel? Nope. She grinned and stretched to kiss me before yelling, "Here we go!"

I looked around the empty hotel room, saying, "I feel like I'm getting off easy."

Her little growl made my mouth curve into a smile, but it straightened when her voice came out reedy and stressed. "What if my dress is all boob and you're like the only one who doesn't think it's obscene?"

"If you came down the aisle topless I would be completely

okay with this. And mine is the only opinion that matters tomorrow."

"Then why did we invite a hundred and sixty-four other people?"

"Hanna. Shut up, right now. Come to my room to get laid."

The line clicked dead, and a few seconds later I heard feet shuffling in front of my door, a long pause, and then a quiet knock.

"Close your eyes," she called from the hallway.

I walked over, closed my eyes tight, and opened the door.

"Keep them closed," she warned.

I squeezed them tighter, obediently.

Her hands moved to my neck and slid up to my face, fumbling in her nervousness before finally managing to tie something around my eyes. And then she fell quiet. I couldn't see her, couldn't feel her.

Reaching out, I found her waist, pulled her to my bare chest. "Tell me what's really going on."

"I don't like not being with you the night before our wedding," she confessed into my skin. "I need you."

Blindly, I ran my hands up her sides, over her shoulders, and along her neck before cupping her face. My fingers met soft silk, and I followed the path of the fabric to a knot at the back of her head.

Hanna had tied a scarf around her eyes, too. Oh, this one.

Laughing, I kissed the top of her head. "So stay with me."

She groaned. "This tradition sucks, but I feel like if there are any traditions I should listen to, it's the ones about how to not mess this marriage up. We can't see each other until tomorrow."

I held her face in my hands, tilting it so I could kiss her. My lips met the tip of her nose first, before traveling south to their target. "There is no way to mess this up," I said, right against her mouth. "Even if we didn't get married to-morrow, you're the love of my life. I'm with you until we both die, at the same time, when I am one hundred and you are ninety-three."

With a quiet laugh, she turned me, guiding me to the bed and carefully pulling me down onto it. She pushed me until I was lying on my back and then climbed over my hips.

"Are your eyes open now?" I asked her, teasing.

"I lifted the blindfold for a second, but they're closed again. *Someone* had to navigate us here safely."

"I mean, I think the rule is the groom can't see the bride, right? You can look at me," I whispered.

She paused. "Really?"

"Yeah, Plum."

After a short hesitation, I heard the shift of her blindfold as she removed it and then the sound of her quiet breaths.

"There you are." She ran a hand up my chest and over my neck, and then a single fingertip traced the shape of my mouth. *"Husband.* Isn't that crazy?"

My skin ignited, hungry. "Hann—"

Her mouth came over mine, shutting me up, lips wet and so fucking full, hands working my boxers down my hips. She licked my neck, her hair tickling my skin as she made her way down my chest, past my stomach . . .

"It's good luck to give head before the wedding," I confirmed when she wrapped her hand around me, licking near the base and dragging her tongue to the tip. "So we're on the right track."

Her giggle vibrated against me as she kissed and sucked, licking me hard as fucking stone in her grip.

"Goddamn," I whispered, hips arching from the bed. "Plum, this blindfold . . . your tongue. *Fuck.*"

She played with me just enough to have me rocking up from the mattress and then I felt her shift and pull her little nightie up over her hips and straddle me.

Her mouth came down against my ear. "No grabbing my boobs."

"Whatever you say," I swore immediately. "Just don't stop."

"You have a gift for bruising boobs. My dress shows boob."

"You mentioned this."

"If you bruise them, no head for a year."

Even though she was probably—I *think*?—joking, the idea made my heart stop for about three beats.

I gave her a reverent "I *promise.*"

She reached for me, rubbing me over the perfect, slippery skin between her legs. My hands made fists around the sheets at my sides.

"Hanna?" I asked in a breathless burst.

Pausing, she asked, "Yeah?"

"Can I grab your hips, though?"

I could feel her go still over me and then start to laugh. "What in the world kind of dress would show my *hips*?"

"Sorry, sorry," I said, laughing. "I'm not thinking. Holy fuck, Plum, just get on my dick."

But she didn't. I could feel the heat of her, so close, and she slowly settled back down on my thighs, her hands running up over my stomach.

"You okay?" I asked, sitting up beneath her and clumsily finding her face again with my hands. "You're freaking out about the dress again?" I tried to surreptitiously swipe my thumbs beneath her eyes to make sure she wasn't crying, but she ducked away.

"I'm not *crying*."

I nodded, going quiet, wanting to tread carefully.

"I'm just nervous," she said.

My chest twisted. "You know that just because we're getting married doesn't mean that anything between us changes, right? We're still Will and Hanna. We're still *us*."

"It feels different already," she said, and slid her fingertips over my lips when I opened my mouth to protest, quickly adding, "I don't mean that in a bad way. I mean, it feels *deeper*. It feels more important. Before, I would look at your body and think, 'Wow, I get to play with *this* all night long!' Now, I look at your body and think, 'Wow, I get to play with this, and *Oh my God what if anything ever happened to him and—*'"

Christina Lauren

"Hanna. Breathe," I said gently from beneath her fingers.

She took a calming breath, sliding her hand down my neck almost as if she was tracing a line to my heart. "I'm only twenty-five," she said after a long pause. "And I know my life would be ruined if I lost you."

The idea of it stabbed sharply into my gut. "You're *never* going to lose me."

She didn't say anything, just drew tiny circles on my chest with her fingertip.

"Plum, come on. We already take such good care of each other. This just makes it official."

Her finger came up again, crossing from one side of my bottom lip to the other, stroking. Thunder pounded through my blood.

"I take care of you?" she asked.

"You do. And when you're not sure how, you ask."

After a few breaths of silence, she said, "Like now?"

I both loved and hated the darkness of the blindfold. I wanted to see her face, but from her voice alone I could imagine it: lip being gently chewed between her teeth, eyes fixed on where her fingers touched my skin with maddening care. This was how we started. She asked, I guided.

"You're not sure how to take care of me right now?"

"I'm just anxious tonight," she whispered. "It helps when you tell me what you want me to do."

My heart seemed to stutter and then explode. It had been a while since we'd played in these roles.

8

"Bring your hips back over me," I instructed, my voice a rough growl.

I felt her shift, and then the heat of her, so intense, barely pressed down on my dick. I bit back a groan.

"Take me in. Slow. Tease me a little."

Her hand came around, steadying as she placed herself over me, rubbing, lowering, bit by bit.

Good holy fuck.

I nearly lost it. "Like that. Like that."

"Will . . ."

A thousand times we'd made love. Maybe more. And it shocked me to no end that I always found myself counting to ten and distracting myself so I wouldn't explode as soon as she took me in.

"Down and up," I said. "Don't tease. Let me feel every inch."

Her breath was a shiver of heat on my neck, her hair tickled along my shoulders, and she did exactly what I asked. But she could have easily taken me in in a single stroke. She was wet as the ocean.

My thoughts spun off the rails over the intensity of it, as it all seemed to hit me in a rush: here we were, on the cusp of this wild fucking adventure—I'd never wanted anything more in my entire life.

And as Hanna moved slowly onto me, and then rocked above, growing confident, forgetting herself, losing herself, I reeled in the truth of that. How many people find the person they ache to touch, to be near, to *belong* to? How many people married their best friend, the person they admired most in the whole world?

I pulled my blindfold off, catching her face just as she fell: eyes fixed on my face, lips parted in a breathless moan. Relief washed over her expression when our eyes met—she needed to see this, see *me*, be steadied by my gaze—and I knew she could read my thoughts as clearly as I could read hers.

Don't trust someone else's tradition, I thought, feeling my body work its way higher, closer. *Trust me. Trust us to find our own path.*

Need and pleasure wrestled their way down my spine, hot and urgent. My fingers dug into her hips, shoving her roughly back and forth over me until I could feel it right there, right at the edge, and her whisper, *I love watching you come*, pushed me over the edge, too.

I came into her with a rough groan, eyes clinging desperately to hers.

"See?" she whispered, face damp with sweat when she pressed it to my neck. "I needed this. Tomorrow is a formality. Right now it feels like we just got married."

"Tomorrow has been a formality ever since you gave me a hand job at a gross student party."

Above me, she giggled.

———

Hanna was gone when I woke up, and her quickly scribbled note left on my pillow—*See you at two!*—made me laugh out loud in the empty room.

My fiancée: what a goddamn romantic.

The morning was packed with a groomsmen breakfast; greeting guests checking into the hotel; my mother and sisters constantly finding me to double-check seating details, delivery instructions, and musician requests. Sensing my need to just take a fucking shower and get ready for my wedding, Jensen swooped in, taking them to find the Command Center (Hanna's mother, Helena), who was more than happy to delegate jobs all damn day.

A hot shower, a good clean shave, and three cups of coffee later, I heard a knock at my hotel room door. A part of me wondered if it might be Hanna, but realized that could only be possible if she had escaped her sister, Liv; her mother; George; and both Chloe and Sara. Aka "the Pride," as Jensen liked to call them, as if they were a pack of lions. If she had somehow managed all that, there would be bodies somewhere, and seeing me before the wedding would be the least of our worries.

"It's me," I heard my nearly-brother-in-law say.

I let Jensen into my suite. He was already dressed, wearing the standard tux, and looking pretty damn great. I'd been with him all day yesterday, but somehow in the packed frenzy of the rehearsal schedule, I hadn't registered that he'd probably lost thirty pounds since I'd last seen him.

"You been working out? You look good, man."

"You're marrying my sister," he said, stepping past me. "Please don't hit on me today."

Laughing, I turned back to the mirror to tie my bow tie.

"Marrying," he repeated, letting out a low whistle.

"I know."

She was going to be my wife. I would get to introduce her that way.

This is my wife.

I couldn't stop rolling the word around in my head. *Wife.* It felt good. It felt substantial. It made me want to climb over her, say it over and over again into her ear, tattooing it in her thoughts.

You're my wife, Plum.

Jensen jerked me from this train of thought when he clapped a hand over my shoulder. *"Married*, Will."

I looked over at him, repeating with a curious smile, "I *know*, Jensen."

"To my little sister." His eyes narrowed as he pointed a mildly threatening finger at me. "That's weird, right?"

We'd had this conversation one other time: over dinner, after Jensen had walked in on us—me beneath the counter, Hanna bent over it with the skirt of her old prom dress shoved above her waist while I went down on her. Luckily he didn't see much . . . but he certainly saw enough to deduce what was going on. In true Hanna fashion, she kept on the dress, put on a pair of sneakers, and made us take her out to pho to smooth over the potential weirdness. Jensen had been surprisingly unfazed until the middle of the meal when he dropped his chopsticks with a tiny clack against his bowl and announced, "Holy shit. *You're going to be my brother.*"

Hanna and I both knew we would be married eventually,

12

but hadn't been quite ready then. At the time, we'd laughed. We were certainly ready *now*.

Jensen walked over to one of the leather chairs near the window and sat down. "Did you ever imagine this day? The day of your wedding, you're getting ready in here with me, she's down the hall getting ready with the Pride?"

I shrugged. "I figured I would find the woman for me, or I wouldn't. I don't think I gave it much thought." I lifted my chin, inspecting my handiwork in the reflection. "Now it seems impossible that in some alternate universe I don't meet up with Hanna. What if she never called me? What if I'd never shown up to run that morning?" Turning to face him, I blinked. "God, that's horrifying."

He could have teased me for this rare sentimental view, but didn't. "I can assure you this wasn't *exactly* what I had in mind when I suggested she call you to hang out," he said, running a finger over an eyebrow. "But here we are. The next time you see her, she's going to be walking down that aisle."

I glanced over at him, having wondered on and off for the past few days how this event felt for him. Hanna and I would be married in the same private garden where Jensen had married his college sweetheart. And where Hanna's older sister, Liv, had married her husband, Rob. Unfortunately, Jensen's marriage to his girlfriend of nine years had lasted only four months.

Jensen broke into my thoughts before I could think of what to say. "Are you imagining how it's going to go down?" he asked.

"Of course. I'm wondering if she'll trip on her way down the aisle or stop mid-journey to hug someone she hasn't seen in years. Hanna *always* surprises me."

"Or if she'll give up walking altogether and just sprint toward you." He laughed quietly. "And it will never stop being weird that you call her Hanna."

"I can't imagine calling her Ziggy," I admitted, and then shivered. "That feels pervy."

"Because it is," he said. "You were seventeen when she was ten. When my little sister was ten, you were sleeping with the mother of one of your bandmates."

I shot him a disgusted look. "Are you trying to make me feel gross?"

"Yeah." He laughed, standing to clap me on the shoulder again just as Bennett and Max pummeled my hotel room door.

Two

Hanna

I stepped back, staring at myself in the mirror.

"That's . . . a lot of white," I mumbled, swiping at the skirt of my dress. Behind me, Mom and Liv gasped emotionally.

"Are we sure I shouldn't have gone for blue? Red? Something that maybe communicates 'I have banged this man daily' versus 'virginal'?"

Mom let out a quiet *"Hanna."*

"What? No one down there is going to see Will in a tux and buy that I didn't climb all over—" I stopped midsentence, catching sight of Chloe behind me. "Are you . . . Oh my God, Chloe. Are—are you *crying*?"

Chloe reached for a box of tissues—one of many placed around the large bridal suite—and pulled one free, using it to carefully dab beneath each of her perfectly lined eyes.

"No," she scoffed. "It's dusty over here."

Liv paused with the curling iron held midair and looked back over her shoulder. "I realize I'm the new kid here, but something tells me that's not normal," she whispered.

I had to bite back a laugh. My sister had only met Chloe on two other, brief occasions, and she already understood that no, when it came to Mrs. Ryan, tears of happiness were *not* a normal thing.

"Well, that's not exactly true," George said to Liv, waving her off before separating a few of the curls she had just placed in my hair. "We could go see the most emotional documentary ever made, and she would leave with clear eyes. But the time a heel broke off one of her red patent Pradas while crossing Seventh? Waterworks."

Chloe laughed, smacking his arm. "Didn't I fire you this morning?"

"Twice," I answered for him. "You fired him on Sara's behalf in the elevator when he referred to you as 'Mistress of the Dark' in front of that priest, and a second time when he offered to help Jensen get dressed later."

Mom let out a tiny squeak of surprise.

"Always so helpful, Hanna, *thank you*," George said, tugging a little too hard on a lock of my hair. "In my defense, he looked *very* busy. I was just trying to be efficient. But as a side note: I should have been warned that Hanna's brother was so adorable, because *really*? Tall, Scandinavian, *and* single? I think I'm the one who's been wronged here."

Liv leaned down and met my eyes in the mirror. "Your friends are weird."

16

"If by weird you mean awesome, then yes," I said, grinning at her before looking back at Chloe. "I love that you're getting emotional at my wedding, though. I feel like I've unlocked a life achievement."

Chloe dabbed her eyes and sniffed into her tissue. "God, what the hell is wrong with me? This is all just so . . . *sweet*."

"Did the BB finally . . . *break* you?" George asked with dramatic awe.

"I will smack you with a hammer," she told him with a glare. "Even in that fancy suit."

"This is awesome for me." Sara came up behind Chloe and hugged her. "Usually *I'm* the one crying."

"Because you're constantly pregnant," Chloe reminded her, reaching back to gently pat Sara's enormous, round belly, carrying Baby Stella Number Two.

"It sure feels that way." Sara kissed Chloe's cheek. "But look." She lifted her chin, meeting my eyes in the mirror. "You've distracted Hanna from being nervous."

"What on earth could you possibly have to be nervous about?" Liv asked, pulling a pin from my hand and giving it to George to tuck into my hair. "You and Will are both thoughtful, intelligent, and conscientious. You guys are going to be *great* at being married."

Our eyes met, and when she smiled at me, I had to bite my lip to keep from getting a little emotional myself.

"If any man ever looks at me the way Will looks at you," George added, "I'll propose, marry, and ask for his

17

babies right there on the spot. Will can barely wait for this wedding. I'm surprised he hasn't convinced you to run off to Vegas."

Liv looked at him over the top of my head "*I'm* not. If he'd ever suggested that, our mother would have cut off all his favorite parts."

In unison, we all turned to look across the room at Mom, who was standing quietly near the window, watching the whole conversation. She gave a decisive nod, and I just about burst out laughing.

George held up an authoritative hand. "Alas, I'm afraid I can't let that happen. I've agreed to let Hanna marry the man of our dreams today, provided she shares all the intimate details. We *need* those parts."

I *was* getting married today. *Me.*

I'd pinch myself, but if this was a dream, I *never* wanted to wake up.

I looked toward the door, in the direction of Will's room, and felt the same tug in my chest I'd felt last night.

"Is it still a surprise where you guys are going tonight?" Sara asked.

"Yes—do *you* know?" I looked at her anxiously but she only shook her head.

"Oh, no," she said, grinning. "Even if I did—which I don't—you wouldn't get it from me. Aren't you the one who told him to surprise you?"

"Yes, but . . . it turns out the idea of a surprise is a lot better than the actual waiting," I admitted. Organizing the wedding had been relatively easy; it was the honeymoon that had thrown a wrench into everything. We'd had it all planned out—a week at a gorgeous house in Maine, absolutely no clothes for any of those days—but then a few interviews I'd thought were long shots turned into sure things, and before I knew it I had interviews scheduled around the country and absolutely no idea where I actually wanted to be. After several discussions and what felt like a hundred scheduling conflicts, we'd decided to postpone the honeymoon. My next interview was in two days, so we'd make the most of the wedding night somewhere local . . . and head home in the morning.

It would be fine. We'd take it one step at a time—one *interview* at a time—and it would work out. New job, new state, new marriage. I just needed to breathe. Will and I were going to be together; *where* and *how* were details that some other Hanna could care about later.

I was about to marry the man of my dreams. Everything else would fall into place.

One wedding down.

One babbling, bumbling bride. One grinning, teary-eyed groom.

Two platinum rings in place.

A *lot* of drunk friends.

And we were married.

Just like I imagined, the wedding and reception were

nothing but a blur. I was grateful for the constant click of cameras, because I would need those photographs to tell me everything else that happened while I walked down the aisle toward Will, my heart trying to climb up my throat and fly from my body into his. I barely noticed the flowers, or the wedding party, or the guests. I barely registered that it was a perfect fall day and that the leaves were fluttering from trees in the most idyllic way imaginable. I barely felt the press of my father's lips to my cheek as he passed my hand over to Will's.

All I could see were Will's intense blue eyes, and the joy that flashed across them as they flickered down to the low neckline of my gown. All I could hear was the deep, reverent rumble of his voice as he repeated his vow to honor, and cherish, and love me for the rest of our lives. And all I could feel was the juxtaposition of cool metal and warm skin as he slid the ring on my finger.

It was all I could process . . . until he kissed me, that is. Because that kiss erased everything that came before it.

You may now kiss your bride.

The world fell away. It really did. It was just us in that tiny spot of land, standing in silence and staring at each other, on the verge of sealing this commitment we'd made.

I couldn't stop smiling.

His hands came up to my face and he let out this quiet, overwhelmed laugh. In his eyes I could practically see the reel of every memory we'd built together: our first run, our first kiss, the first time we'd made love, our first fight, the weekend he proposed—twice—and each moment of laughter and quiet between us since.

And then my husband bent, covering my lips with his. I should have known better than to expect a gentle peck. The kiss went on, and on, to the growing hoots and hollers of our friends. But despite their shared joy, I could have left the entire celebration then and there. I could have taken Will's hand and pulled him into a closet and kissed him for days, just sealing this most important promise for hours.

After the *I do*'s, we walked out into the garden with its towering trees and twinkling lights to the sound of our family and friends' cheers. My cheeks ached from smiling and I tightened my grip on Will's hand, because he was the only thing anchoring me to the ground. Without his steady touch I was sure I'd simply float away, disappearing into the night sky like a balloon.

I was grateful I'd listened to advice reminding me that in twenty years, I'd only remember *him*. Because it was true: his eyes barely strayed from me all night, and when they did it was because he'd pulled me close and his hands took over, roaming carefully over my arms, my back, my sides. The entire reception felt like one long, drawn-out session of foreplay, and by the time I threw the bouquet, I was practically vibrating to be alone with him.

It was only when we were in the town car and on our way to Will's surprise wedding-night location that we had a moment to breathe.

"I can't believe I made it through that entire thing without screwing up," I said. I'd been smiling nonstop for hours now. My cheeks were sore and my rapid heartbeat left a constant, giddy feeling in my chest.

"I don't know about the *entire* thing," Will teased, easily evading a slug to the arm. "I'm kidding." With a finger under my chin, he tilted my face up to him. "Didn't I tell you everything would be perfect?"

"You did," I said, stretching to nip at his jaw. "Apparently big social gatherings where I am prominently featured stress me out a little. Who knew?"

He laughed.

"Hey, guess what?"

"What?"

"You're my favorite."

He returned the sentiment with a kiss to my lips, and one kiss turned into another until we heard the driver clear his throat from the front seat. With a self-conscious laugh, I put a little more space between us. I wasn't going to get carried away in the back of a car on our way to the hotel; I had the entire night with him. I planned on savoring every moment.

"Did you notice how much champagne Jensen had?" I asked.

My oldest brother might have the air of the Responsible Sibling, but he did play in a band with Will, after all. I was pretty sure Jensen wasn't quite as innocent as he always claimed to be.

"I saw him talking to that redhead who works in your lab," Will said, nodding. "Think he might have a hard time finding his way home alone." He leaned over to press a kiss to my cheek, my chin, before making his way to my jaw. "Maybe I won't be the only one getting lucky tonight."

I grimaced. "I'm going to pretend you didn't just make a reference to my brother getting laid on my wedding night." Will laughed against my throat, his warm breath bringing goose bumps to the surface of my skin. "We both know my brother doesn't have sex, because, *gross*," I added, trying to swallow back my anxious chatter. "Why don't you just start talking about how handsy my dad was with my mom tonight?"

Will pulled back, staring down at me in amusement. "How much champagne did *you* have tonight?" he asked, fingers curling around my hip. "You're not asleep on the floor, so I'm guessing it wasn't a lot."

"Liv cut me off at half a glass. She said it was her gift to you and that you could thank her at Christmas."

Will laughed and we both turned toward the window as the car slowed and then rolled to a gentle stop. He slid across the seat and then turned back to me with a grin.

"You ready?" he asked, and I wondered if two words had ever been packed with so much meaning.

Was I ready? Not in a million years. I was barely prepared to handle Will Sumner on an average day, never mind in a hotel room, in a tuxedo, on our wedding night, and with that *look* in his eye . . .

It was a look that suggested I was something to eat. It was a look that told me I didn't stand a chance. The door opened and Will stepped out, quickly turning to offer me his hand. I followed, and was instantly greeted by the sights and sounds of Rowes Wharf and the city just beyond.

"So this is what you've been planning," I said, looking from the boats rocking gently in the harbor to the beautifully illuminated building in front of us. "You kept this place a secret from me, you little sneak."

He grinned. "You said to surprise you."

"How in the world . . . ?" I started, but just shook my head, hit by a wave of nostalgia so big it took my words away. I'd been to the Boston Harbor Hotel as a child and always wanted to come back, but had no idea how he knew any of this. "Did my mom tell you about this place?"

"Well, she did help me organize things a little, but no, she didn't tell me. *You* did," he said, placing his hand on my lower back and leading us both to the lobby doors.

"I tell you approximately three hundred random things a day. I have no idea how you manage to retain even a fraction of them."

Our bags had been delivered earlier in the day, so once we had our room keys, we headed straight for the elevators.

Pressing the call button, Will bent to place a lingering kiss against my cheek. "Your dad brought you here for afternoon tea when you were eight, and your mother made you wear a terrible dress and tights that kept—if I have my Hanna-isms correct—*creeping into your fancy parts?* I might be paraphrasing, of course."

I laughed at the memory. "I hated that dress. It was Liv's, and the zipper was all jagged and would snag in my hair." He gave me a slow nod to tell me he remembered all of this . . . and my insides warmed. "There were rose petals on the tablecloths."

"Pink," he added, rubbing slow circles on my back with his palm.

I nodded, eyes locked on his before dropping to his gorgeous mouth. I wanted to kiss that mouth, taste it, stretch out across a giant bed while it tasted *me*. We'd made love just last night and yet it still felt like it'd been too long.

"I feel like I barely got to talk to you today," I whispered. "How weird is that? It was our wedding, we were next to each other all night, and yet it feels like we spent most of the day talking to other people."

"I felt the same way," he said, and the low rumble of his voice vibrated down my spine. "Between the guests and the pictures, your family, my family, and the guys all stealing you for dances . . . I just stared at you all night."

I pulled him down for another kiss and felt him hum against my mouth. "Would you be interested in some alone time now?" I asked. "I'd like to show you how much I like your surprise."

"I'm a little torn between wanting to stare at you in

this dress some more, and wanting to tear it off you." The elevator doors opened and we stepped inside, shifting to the back to make room for a few others, who smiled at us and murmured their congratulations.

Every time I remembered that Will was my *husband* now, tiny bombs went off inside my chest.

I pressed my face to his shoulder, breathing him in as the elevator began to climb. He smelled amazing; the scent of orchids that had filled the entire reception clung to him. I felt light-headed for a moment. Gone were any nerves and exhilaration, and sheer fucking *want* raced through my veins.

I did a quick check to make sure nobody was paying attention, and then pushed up onto my toes so I could whisper into his ear.

"I know we head home early tomorrow," I said, already dreading the alarm that would go off at eight in the morning to get us to the airport on time. "So we need to make the best use of our time. Bed, floor, couch . . . I want you to take me everywhere." I paused, adding even more quietly, "I want to *feel* you everywhere."

Will straightened with a quick intake of air and looked around us. "Christ, Hanna."

"What? I'm whispering."

Will bit back a laugh. "Have you ever actually heard yourself whisper? It's like a stage whisper, done only for comedic effect and meant to be heard by the people all the way in the back."

I shook my head. "No way." Pointing to my chest, I added, "Super subtle."

Will's continued laughter was cut short as the doors opened on the second floor, and everyone shifted to let an older couple step out. I hated to admit it, but if the looks everyone gave us over their shoulders were any indication, Will was right . . . they'd heard everything.

As we started moving again, Will leaned in and pressed his mouth to my ear. "But honestly, I like the sound of all of this."

"I have a list and want to make sure we get to everything."

"You have a *list*."

I looked at him, blinking. "You don't?"

"Hanna," he said, laughing. "You are amazing."

A chime signaled we'd reached our floor and the doors opened. I'd barely taken a step forward when he reached for me, swooping me up in his arms and laughing as my surprised screech rang up and down the empty hall.

"You're carrying me?"

"I'm carrying you."

I looped my arms around his neck. "I thought you weren't a fan of traditions."

I could hear his footsteps against the plush carpet, but couldn't seem to drag my eyes away from his face. I was fascinated by his mouth and his lashes and the way my fingers slipped so easily through the back of his hair.

"Some traditions must be based on research," he said,

27

smiling down at me. "Everyone who has ever done this before me surely discovered how heroic it feels."

I gazed up at him. "I'm not tiny, and there are about forty pounds of pearls on this dress. Look at you: you're not even winded. I am impressed."

Shrugging with me in his arms, he added more quietly, "Also, your tits look amazing all squeezed together like that. It's win-win."

I barked out a surprised laugh. "The truth comes out."

Will stopped in front of a room, somehow managing to slip the keycard into the lock and turn the handle, letting the door swing open in front of us.

"Well, Mrs. Sumner-Bergstrom, here we are." He paused, pressing a soft kiss against my mouth to mark the moment, and then carried me over the threshold.

It hit me all over again: We were married. Will was my husband—*my husband*.

For the past three months, no matter how busy our lives were—at work, at home, with friends—some wedding-related question would manage to work its way into every conversation. I was glad I'd taken everyone's advice, reminding myself that it was *just a day*, and so much of it would go by in a blur. I didn't remember much about the flowers or place settings at the reception, or even what we ate. But I did remember Will's face when I saw him for the first time at the end of that aisle, waiting for me. I remembered how happy he looked as he watched me come toward him, how every bit of self-consciousness I felt about my dress or my boobs or being in front of all these people just slipped away when I saw his eyes roam the length of my body. I would have raced down the aisle naked if he'd asked me to. His voice shook when he said his vows, and I'll never forget the tears in his eyes when he said *I do.*

"I'm ready to have sex now," I told him, unwilling to wait another minute.

Will smiled and shook his head, taking the final steps that would lead us into the suite's master bedroom. "Life will never be boring with you around, Plum."

I'm sure our room was gorgeous—plush carpet, wide windows, and beautiful furniture, just like the rest of the hotel—but I never saw any of it, unable to pull my lips from the side of his neck while he lowered me to the bed, my dress crinkling between us.

Will reached over and switched on the crystal lamp next to the bed, and there he was, hovering above me.

"I love you," I said.

"I love you, too."

I was so ready for this wedding night . . . but he wasn't moving. I waited, blinking off to the side before peering back up at him again. "Everything okay?"

"Everything is fucking perfect."

Another moment passed. I took in his soft smile, the way his eyes moved over every part of my face before focusing on my mouth. "Then . . . what are you doing?"

"Looking at you. Looking at my *wife.*"

Christina Lauren

"That's not really getting us any closer to having sex."

Will laughed and shook his head. "We're *married*, Hanna," he said, and it sounded like he was still marveling at it, too . . .

"Say, I was *wondering* what you were doing in this tuxedo." I wrapped his tie around my fist and tugged on it, bringing him closer. "Unless you're just a really, really snappy dresser. But then, you have this ring on your finger, too . . ."

"I want to be sweet with you," he said, palm curving over my shoulder and slipping down between my breasts. There was a weight there, a pressure to his touch I could feel even through the thin layers of fabric. Despite the softness in his voice, it screamed of possession, of lust. "I *feel* like I should be sweet tonight."

The delicate lamp threw shadows across his face and I pulled on his tie again, stopping when his mouth was just above mine. "You're always sweet to me, Will. You make me feel loved and respected and cherished, every single day. I love that side of you."

His smile widened, and I could hear the edge of laughter in his voice when he spoke into the darkness.

"I'm sensing a big *but* in there somewhere, Plum."

"But we have *eight hours* before we need to be up."

His brows lifted in amusement. "Eight *whole* hours."

"That's right. So you can be sweet the second time."

It was all he needed to hear. Watching Will lose his restraint was like watching a fuse burn down. He lunged

30

forward and any space that separated us was gone just like that. The heat of his body radiated along mine and I groaned, pushing his jacket off.

"Clothes," I mumbled between kisses, between the taste of his tongue and the sharp bite of his teeth. "Off." I pulled on his shirt, fingers fumbling with buttons and his tie, in search of skin.

Will nodded, helping me free him of his shirt before sitting me up just enough to unzip my dress and pull it down. I wanted to tell him to be careful, to remind him how many hours I endured shopping with my mother for this dress, that the fabric was delicate and could easily tear. But I'd never cared less about clothes in my life. I suddenly felt frantic, like when school and work got to be too much and I thought my muscles might burst from my skin if I didn't get out and run, just *move*.

It took some maneuvering on both our parts, but with a final tug Will managed to pull the fabric over my hips and down my legs. I bolted up onto my knees, lips seeking skin and greedy hands trying to drag him back down to me.

"I love you so much," I said between kisses. "Today was so perfect, this . . . tonight . . . all of it. You."

I could feel his smile against my mouth, our kiss clumsy with teeth and whispered words and so much happiness that we were finally here, together.

"You have no idea how long I've waited for this," he said, a gentling hand on either side of my face as he held me.

"Since the night you came to my apartment?" I asked, but he was already shaking his head.

"Earlier. Maybe since that day on the trail? In your brother's baggy sweatshirt and—"

"And my terrible bra?" I said, laughing against his jaw. "It will never stop being funny that you had Chloe take me shopping. You must have been mortified."

"You had to keep holding your boobs and it made me so sad for them. I wanted to offer to hold them for you—offer my *support*—apologize for how mean you were being to them," he said, swiping a thumb over my nipple.

"God, I would have lost my mind," I said, my giggle turning into a soft moan as he increased the pressure. There was one kiss, then a second, one to each corner of my mouth before he tilted my head, thumb pressed to the bottom of my jaw.

He moved lower and I heard him swear when he realized what I was wearing, his finger coming up to touch the delicate lace barely covering my breasts.

"Chloe," I said, no further explanation needed.

He swallowed and reached up to wipe his forehead with the back of his arm, then took a long, heavy breath, eyes never leaving where my breasts were barely restrained by the soft material. "Remind me of this when her birthday comes around," he said.

"I'm basically spilling out of it," I told him.

"Exactly my point," he said, gently coaxing me back

and pressing me to the bed. My legs fell open and he moved to his knees, hips between my parted thighs and his silhouette framed by the large windows. I looked up at him, struck in that moment by how much bigger he was than me, the way his wide shoulders and broad back were enough to blot out the city lights behind him.

I reached up, feeling the shape of him still in his pants, and squeezed, a little too tight, just the way he liked it.

With a grunt he lowered his head, leaning to lick at the hollow of my throat. The ceiling blurred and I closed my eyes, lost to the sensation of his mouth and teeth, the scrape of his chin, the pressure where his fingers worked to make room for himself inside my body.

I gasped, arching my spine against the bed and dragging my nails down his shoulder and across his back, hard, but not too hard. Not sure if he was ready yet. Will liked for it to hurt sometimes, asked for it. It was that thing that pushed him over the edge when he was so close he couldn't catch his breath or think or even ask for what he wanted. He only knew he wanted *more*.

Will must have seen the question in my eyes because he swallowed and took a shaky breath. "Make it hurt," he said.

I twisted my fingers in his hair, desperate and deep and just rough enough that his hips shot forward in surprise.

I rolled Will to his back and lifted my leg to straddle his hips. In the soft light I registered the surprise on his face and the way he dragged his teeth over his bottom lip when I reached up and unfastened my bra.

Cool air spilled across my breasts and my nipples hardened. Will freed himself of his pants and maneuvered my panties down and off my body. His skin was warm beneath me, his thighs firm and covered in soft hair. His hard cock rested against his stomach.

I pushed up onto my knees and positioned him where I wanted, smoothing him against me, teasing him.

"Do you want this?" I asked.

He nodded against the pillow, thumbs pressed into my hips, fingers gripping my ass. I lowered myself

slowly

    slowly

        until he was fully inside.

Will groaned helplessly, thrusting up into me while I moved over him. His hands reached to cup my breasts and lifted, squeezed them together before he sat up and took a nipple into his mouth.

"Will."

He moaned around me, sucking harder before releasing it, his tongue drawing circles around the tip. He was so deep, and all I could think about or feel or hear was him. His stomach was slick with sweat where it moved against mine, his thighs firm against my ass. His fingers where he held me down and lifted me up slipped as he held me tighter, tried to move us faster.

With a groan, he flipped us over, throwing me to my

back, his head down and hair fallen over his forehead. He watched where he moved inside of me, in and out. Harder. Faster.

An eternity, but never long enough.

"Fuck, Plum," he said, kissing me until it was too much and my mouth was practically raw. With one hand he lifted my leg and pushed it to my chest.

"Jesus *fuck*," he said, pistoning his hips faster now, each thrust pushing against something inside me that had me seeing stars.

I reached up, fingers grappling for the headboard, needing something to hold on to. Each snap of his hips pushed me further up the mattress and deeper inside that place in my head where static roared and the growing tension inside my lower belly—the friction and heat between my legs—became impossible to ignore.

"Will," I breathed, gasping against his open mouth. I was going to come and I needed to come with him, *feel* him coming inside me and then again and again, on my breasts and my stomach, my lips.

Will reached for the edge of the mattress and pushed my leg farther into my chest and that was it. Heat exploded between my legs and ricocheted through every part of me. My toes curled, and I was coming so hard I couldn't cry out or even say his name. He rocked into me one last time, so deep it took the breath from my lungs and I could feel him, muscles tense as he came inside me.

Will fell back to the bed and pulled me with him, cradling me into his side. "Holy shit."

I blinked up at the ceiling, waiting for my breathing to return to normal. My bones were rubber; air cooled my fevered skin. I looked over to Will before reaching for the clock on the side of the bed. Six hours, twenty-two minutes to go. Not bad.

Sitting up, I filled two glasses from a bottle of chilled water on the bedside table, emptied mine in a single long draft, and climbed up onto Will's lap.

His eyes moved down my naked body before he took the other glass from my hand. I watched him drink, marveling at his throat as he swallowed, his bare chest, his messy hair. This body? Was mine. Once he'd finished, I took the empty glass and pushed him back down to the pillows.

"Now," I said, raising a single brow, "about that list . . ."

THREE

Will

"Are you sure you don't mind postponing the honeymoon?" On the couch at my side, Hanna turned her face up to me, squinting in the late-afternoon sun that streamed through our living room window. "Are you worried it will feel sort of . . . anticlimactic?"

A wild wedding, a sleepless wedding night, another interview checked off the list, and there we were: one week later, already back in our apartment, back in our day-to-day life.

There was something reassuring about taking the monumental step but then immediately falling back into pace with the rest of life. It reaffirmed what I'd told Hanna all along: The *us* beneath it all didn't have to change. We could still be exactly who we were before. Married folk definitely lazed around in their underwear on a Saturday afternoon.

"I'm fine waiting." I kissed her nose, pulling her closer. "As long as you don't tack on any more interview trips in the meantime."

Our rescheduled honeymoon was already booked for a

Christina Lauren

little over a month after the wedding—late October—with a job-interview-free week beforehand to pack, finish up anything important in the lab, and hold any critical meetings. I wanted as much time with Hanna at home as possible.

I felt her response to this in her tiny hesitation, saw it in her small wince. "Hanna?"

"Not even for Caltech?" she asked sweetly.

What an odd feeling: to be fed up, to want to roll my eyes when my wife—holy fuck, my *wife*—received an interview request from Cal-fucking-tech.

"And when would it be?" I asked.

"Late October? We would still have a few days to get ready for the trip." Her smile was so sweet, so genuinely hopeful, how could I possibly tell her no?

How would I, anyway? This was her career, her dream. Hanna was being courted by academic institutions all over the world. Her first interviews had been local: Princeton, Harvard, MIT, Johns Hopkins. But then the invitations had spread: Cal, Stanford. Max Planck in Germany. Oxford in the UK. And now, Caltech.

The thing was, we hadn't really talked about how it would be if she wanted to move. We were in a holding pattern, stuck in a conversation on pause.

I kissed her nose again in answer.

"Does that mean yes?" she asked, studying me with a little smile.

"It means I would never tell you no, Plum. I think you should visit the universities you want to consider." Kissing

38

her mouth, I asked, "Do you feel like you have a favorite yet?"

She scrunched her nose at this. "I mean, not really?"

I watched her blink a few times, the tiny panic a little flutter in her breath. This process was a daunting one. I remembered being at that point myself: out of my post-doc and ready to tackle the next phase of my career, yet unable to believe, no matter how good my publications were, or how many job interviews I got, that I'd be able to hack it day in and day out running a lab. Research is scary. Academic research is cutthroat.

It's one of the reasons I went into industry: I trusted my ability to determine whether a technology could be profitable and how to get it there more than I trusted my ability to come up with something innovative in its own right.

Likewise, Hanna knew her own strengths: her technical creativity was nearly limitless, and she had a rare ability to easily integrate everything she read into the broader scientific context. She would make an amazing professor. I simply worried it would take more out of her than she anticipated.

Best to cross that bridge when we come to it.

She took a deep breath, looking past me up at the ceiling. "The head of the department at Caltech sounds amazing. She seems really happy. I sort of imagined this department full of old, awkward nerd dudes, but apparently it isn't like that at all."

"No?"

"Well, at least not primarily. I'm sure there are still *plenty* of awkward nerd dudes." Shaking her head, she continued, "Her name is Linda Albert. She made me feel like I would have time for things outside of the lab, which I *never* hear on these calls. She asked about you, about your job and how you're taking this whole interview process."

"She did?"

Hanna nodded, sipping from her mug of tea before stretching to return it to the coffee table. She snuggled back into my arms. "I told her you were amazing. I told her you're the most competent man I know."

I pulled away, gazing down at her. A smile tugged at my mouth. "Did you say it like that?"

Hanna shook her head, confused. "Like what?"

"Like there are categories of competence, and a competent *man* is a lesser category."

She laughed, holding up her hands. "No, no, I—"

I bent, tickling her waist, and she fell back on the couch. "As in, I'm not a bad driver . . . for a dog."

Laughing harder, she wrestled against my invading, tickling fingers.

"Basically, you told the head of biotech at Caltech that your husband is a water-skiing squirrel."

She grinned up at me, and I slowed my assault, bending instead to kiss her, to slide my lips on top of hers, feel her closed mouth opening against mine.

I moved my hand up from her waist, resting my first two fingers just above her collarbone, feeling her pulse there.

"Love you," she murmured lazily, eyes closed.

"I love you, too."

I watched her relax on our couch, listened to the sounds of cars and people outside. The early autumn breeze slid in through the window, cooling as night approached.

"It's so good in the quiet," Hanna said.

"It's *always* good." I smiled, absently humming a song I knew she liked lately, listening to the rhythm of her breath.

The pad of her finger traced the plum tattoo on my arm, and slid lower, to the black *H* on my hip, her favorite.

"What do you want to do tonight?" she asked.

I shrugged, running my fingers up through the soft tangle of her hair. "This. Be married. Maybe put on a movie. Order some dinner. Go to bed and fuck for a while."

"Can I switch up the order of that a little?" she asked, fingers sliding just under the waistband of my boxers.

But as if the universe heard our plans and laughed out loud at this bullshit, the pounding of footsteps sounded outside in the hallway before a symphony of fists met our door.

Hanna startled, bolting upright. "What the hell?" she asked, turning to look at me.

"Bergstrom-Sumnerses!" Max shouted from the hallway. "Open thy door!"

"I think they went with Sumner-Bergstrom," I heard George correct.

My stomach dropped.

Before the wedding, we'd had no time for parties: Hanna was traveling, I was working, life was too busy for the requisite bachelor and bachelorette shenanigans. And to be frank, neither of us much needed them anyway; we didn't need any particular send-off for the single days—much to the friends' dramatic, and *vocal*, disappointment. In the past week, we'd fallen back into routine and planned for a quiet post-wedding weekend at home. Hanna wanted us to be together at our apartment before another flurry of work trips began.

The friends knew this.

They knew we were home.

Shit.

They had promised us a party when the wedding was done.

"I think I know what this is." I stood, walking to the front door and not giving one single fuck that I was wearing nothing but my boxers. They wanted to come here unannounced? They'd get what they got.

The door swung open to reveal Chloe and Bennett, Max and Sara, and George, holding an armful of booze.

"*Surprise!*" everyone yelled in unison.

Everyone but George, who was staring at my boxers. "It's like you knew I was coming over."

"Wow. Hey, guys," I said flatly.

"You have no choice but to let us get you drunk and have our collective way with you," Chloe said, holding up an armful of lacy garments. "Some of these are for Hanna, but most of them George picked out for you."

"Well then hell, come in," I said, stepping aside.

Max and Bennett lingered in the hall, looking guilty. I

42

raised my brows, looking at them expectantly. "You guys coming in or . . . ?"

They hesitated, sharing a glance between them.

"The wives thought . . ." Max began, taking in my minimalist outfit.

"No, hey, it's cool," I said, giant fake smile in place. "The new wife and I were just about to enjoy some newlywed sex, but, see, this is *way* better."

"Look," Bennett said, "we probably should have called first, but . . . Chloe."

"Called first?" I laughed, clapping their shoulders roughly and pulling them inside. These dicks were getting so drunk they wouldn't be able to walk home. "No need to call! You're welcome to come into my house and hang out with me and my new bride in our underwear any fucking time."

Max slunk in, laughing quietly. "Well, shit."

"First shots for these gentlemen," I said, putting an arm around each of their shoulders. "They'd like to get these here festivities done started!"

Chloe followed George into the kitchen, while Sara went to the living room, hugging a still shell-shocked Hanna and putting on some music. An upbeat rock song filtered through the apartment, and they both came back to where the rest of us had gathered.

Hanna slipped her arms around my waist, meeting my eyes. "What just happened?" she asked me through a laugh.

In her expression I could see the question: *Are we game for this?*

And in truth, we had a lifetime of quiet Saturday nights together. The looks of excitement on our friends' faces were hard to resist.

I bent, kissing her once. "I fear tonight is going to get out of hand very quickly," I said against her lips.

She laughed. "I think you may be right."

Coming out with a tray of tequila shots, Chloe handed one each to me, Hanna, and George, and two each to Bennett and Max.

"Good woman," I said to Chloe.

Sara happily unscrewed the cap to her water bottle and Chloe ushered us all in closer. "Everyone get in here, raise your damn glasses." A cluster of glasses clinked together. "To the newlyweds: Will and Hanna Sumner-Bergstrom. Get ready for a lifetime of being badass motherfuckers."

The tequila warmed a path from my lips to my gut, and I glanced at Hanna, catching the first shudder as it made its way through her, followed by her disgusted wince.

"Oh, God, that's horrible," she moaned.

"Then you just need to do more," George said, jogging to the kitchen and returning a couple of minutes later with another round.

"This is madness," I told them. "You got here five minutes ago and we're standing in the hallway doing *shots* like a bunch of fratty idiots."

Bennett agreed with a nod, but took his third shot anyway.

"You failed to be tortured on a stag night," Max pointed

out, lifting his glass. "Bennett had one in Vegas. You all held mine at that dive bar in the Meatpacking District."

"An apt description, if memory serves," Bennett added. "I think more than a few patrons had sex in the bathroom that night."

"Besides, when was the last time we all got hammered together?" Chloe asked.

The group fell silent.

"I think never?" Hanna offered, tossing back the next shot before gagging and squeezing her eyes closed. "I don't think I like tequila."

I watched her—cheeks flushed, lips wet from the booze—and walked into the kitchen, grabbing a lime and the saltshaker.

"Here," I said, pulling her close.

"Oh, *yes*," George cooed from somewhere behind us. "Only a few minutes in and we're in body shot land."

"Lick my neck," I told her, and she was obviously already tipsy because she did it in front of our friends without hesitation. "Shake some salt there."

I felt the cascade of salt down my bare chest.

"Okay," Hanna said. "And then?"

"Lick the salt, take the shot, and suck this lime from my mouth."

"Can we all please take note here that Will is still in only his boxers?" Sara called out from across the room, where she turned up the volume on the stereo. "Is anyone else a little uncomfortable?"

"My Snapchat feed is having a banner fucking day," George mumbled, snapping a picture before I reached over and knocked the phone out of his hand.

Hanna's mouth came up over my neck to loud whistles and clapping, and then she took the shot and leaned forward, sucking the lime wedge from between my lips.

Well, fuck.

She moved back and I watched her suck at the wedge, smiling at me with her eyes.

"Better?" I asked.

Pulling it away, she shook her head. "Nope, still gross."

She kissed me and tasted like tequila and lime. I could taste her lips all day and chase her for more.

But she put a hand on my chest, pushing slightly. "Go put on some pants. You're . . . a little into this." Nodding to my boxers, she grinned up at me and I realized I was sporting half-wood standing in the middle of my apartment, surrounded by my friends.

Bennett laughed, turning away.

"Fuck you guys," I said, punching his shoulder before walking back to the bedroom.

⚬══════⚬

In no time at all everyone but Sara was falling-down drunk. Even Hanna, whom I'd seen tipsy on but a few occasions, would only stop giggling when overtaken by a bout of body-jerking hiccups. The coffee table was covered with novelty straws, playing cards, shot glasses, and beer bottles. A bag of tortilla chips sat several inches away from a nearly empty bowl, and no one seemed to care that the stretch of table between the two was marked by frequent dollops of salsa.

"Hanna. What's the deal with the job hunt?" Bennett asked, in true drunk-Bennett proactive displeasure.

Hanna held up three fingers. "I have two more inter-views."

"Where?" Sara asked, pushing a glass of water closer to her.

My adorably drunk wife worked to focus on her fingers, ticking off, "Berkeley. Caltech."

Chloe scowled. "If you move to the West Coast, I will make a gun out of this," she said, drunkenly brandishing a tiny straw before searching the rest of the cluttered table, "and these peanuts and this glass and shoot you in the dick, Will."

I winced at the visual. "Wow—" I began.

"*In the dick*, Will."

"Okay, wow. That's . . . vivid. I'm not the one with the job interviews."

"But you have a say in it," Max reminded me.

"It doesn't matter." I waved a drunken hand, feeling a quiet panic start to surge in me. "Hanna will basically live in the lab anyway."

"Whoa." Her head lolled to face me. "That's not fair."

"It's true, though." I leaned an elbow on the table, rest-ing my cheek on my fist. It was as though I'd had a sheet over the pile of worries building in my mind, and the alcohol lifted it and tossed it to the side. "I want you to get a straightforward teaching job so I'll actually see you. But you're not looking at those."

Her head jerked back, eyes narrowing. "I don't *want* a 'straightforward teaching job.' I want to run a *lab*, too."

"I know." I shrugged. "I get it. It's just the choice you're making, though."

The tiny part of my brain that wasn't drunk sent up a warning flag. A small voice in the back of my head told me I was being a dick.

But I didn't care. It was true, wasn't it? The idea of Hanna taking a faculty position at a big research institution scared me. It was one of the reasons I hadn't taken such a job myself: the pressure to publish in high-ranking journals is killer. It leaves time for nothing else.

Until she was tenured—for a matter of *years*—her entire life would have to be her lab.

Besides, she had interviews all over the damn place and still hadn't given me any indication where she wanted to go. We could be uprooting our entire home in a matter of months to move across the country, and I had no idea of where yet.

We were married a week ago and already I was preparing myself to come second to her career.

"Let's play more Truth or Dare," George suggested, loudly redirecting us from an incoming argument.

"It was your turn," Bennett said to Hanna.

"Fine," Hanna said, glaring at me, "but we aren't done discussing this."

"Can you wait until we're gone, though?" Bennett asked. "Christ, I'm sorry I asked."

"Says the man who fight-fucks his wife in public every bleeding day," Max said.

Hanna flapped her hands in front of her, bringing our attention back to the game. "Truth or dare, Mr. Sumner-Bergstrom."

I leaned forward, smiling. "Oooh, dare."

Hanna couldn't hold in her delighted giggle. "I dare you to kiss George."

We all turned to look at George, who had gone as white as a sheet.

"What?" he said. "*Wait*. What did she just say?"

"Come here," I growled, playing it up for the crowd.

George shook his head in disbelief, chanting, "Oh my God, oh my God . . ."

Grabbing a rough handful of his hair, I leaned in, tilting his head to bring it closer to mine. His eyes went wide.

I nipped at his bottom lip with my teeth. "Breathe, George."

"Are you going to ruin me?" he asked, voice thin and hoarse.

"I'm sure as fuck gonna try," I told him, and then leaned forward, covering his mouth with mine, and—fuck it, I was drunk—sliding my tongue inside for a tiny little tease.

Against me, George seemed to melt, his mouth still open when I pulled away.

Everyone cheered loudly.

49

"You okay?" I asked him.

"I will be okay *forever* now," he said, dazed.

I leaned back, glancing over at Hanna, who looked like she was going to fucking *eat* me. I moved close to her, kissing her once. "Was that okay?"

She nodded, attempting to look unaffected. "Not bad."

Her neck was flushed, breaths short and choppy. My kinky little wife.

"Are you so wet right now?" I asked quietly.

She nodded again, mouth curling in a slow-growing smile.

"Still mad at me?" I asked.

Her eyes cooled as she remembered. "I don't want to talk about it now. I'm too drunk."

I hadn't actually been that worried about the whole thing until she said this. Hanna and I argued in thirty-second bites. One of us would say something and the other would disagree and we would decide it was worth discussing, or not.

Because Hanna hated conflict more than anything.

We didn't yell.

We didn't ask to talk about something later.

We just didn't fight, but part of me really *wanted* to.

My stomach felt sour and queasy.

———

What felt like hours of debauchery followed. Chloe and Sara had planned all manner of adolescent entertainments, including a boisterous game of Bullshit (Max won), a widely inaccurate game of Velcro darts (there was no clear winner there), and a game of Never Have I Ever that had us all worried Chloe or Bennett would draw blood on our new Persian rug.

By the time 3 a.m. arrived, everyone was staring dully at the ceiling, lying in a tangle, half our limbs beneath the coffee table.

"We should go," Bennett slurred, pushing himself up with obvious effort. "We only have thirty hours before we need to reestablish a plausible executive presence."

"I'm going to be hungover," Chloe moaned. "Who can I pay to dial back time and undo three of those tequila shots? Maybe four."

Sara, who had been asleep in our bed, walked out, stretching. "I just called a couple cabs. Let's go, drunkies."

At the door, Hanna stopped them, hugging everyone in turn. "Thanks for this. It was actually super fun just to be stupid with you guys for a few hours."

"We're all chuffed for you," Max said, weaving in the doorway.

"And you never get to just hang out at home with friends," Chloe added. "I'm glad you took a night to slow down a little."

With a pat to Hanna's head, she turned, leading the rest of them out of our house.

Hanna turned to me, leaning against my shoulder. "Do I really work like that? All the time?"

I shrugged, kissing the top of her head. "Sort of," I said, my frustration at her from earlier diffused.

It was one of the things I admired about Hanna: she was

taking the academic world by storm. But it was also the thing that challenged my vision of our future the most. As much as I hated to admit it, I loved the idea of Hanna at home with me at night, Hanna someday pregnant with our child, Hanna always with me when I was away from my own job.

She was never meant to be a wife first and foremost, and I *knew* that—had always known it, and fuck, I never expected to *want* that in a woman—but some unevolved part of me wanted more of her time and her focus before I'd even lost it.

"I thought I fixed that last year," she said. "Jensen got all up in my business. I thought I got out of the lab, got a man, got some action."

I turned us both, leading us to the bathroom to brush our teeth. "Old habits die hard."

She shook her head as she shoved her toothbrush in her mouth, squeezing her eyes closed. "I don't want to talk about it tonight."

Her words were muffled and she brushed roughly. But then she said anyway: "You made me mad when you said I should get a teaching job."

Bending to spit, I asked, "What's wrong with a teaching job? It would probably be a more regular schedule, which would be better for *us*."

She looked at me, mouth foamy, eyes wide and glassy, and then bent to spit after me, rinsing her mouth. "You're going to make me feel guilty over this?"

"No," I told her, but I had to be honest. "But I guess I

have feelings about it after all. I feel like I have no idea what the plan is. Yeah, I can work from anywhere, but it would be nice to have a general region in mind."

She wiped her mouth on a towel and stood there, eyes closed as she took a deep breath. "Okay. We aren't doing this right now. My brain is all blah blah drunk."

With a decisive nod, she looked back at me. "Putting this aside."

I took a step closer, bending to kiss her. "Putting this aside."

When my tongue touched hers, she pulled back, laughing. "Oh my God, I just remembered I made you kiss George."

"You did."

"He liked it."

This made me laugh. "You think so?"

"Did *you*?"

"I mean, it wasn't *terrible.* But it also wasn't you."

I followed her into the bedroom and between the covers. "Do you think he's in love with you?"

I shook my head. "No. I think maybe he just really wants me to fuck him?"

Hanna laughed and climbed over me, kissing my bare chest. "I bet he'd love to do this." She moved lower, pulling my boxers down and off, tossing them onto the floor of our bedroom. Her mouth came up against the head of my cock, tongue teasing. "I love the way you feel on my tongue." She sucked me, drunk and bold. "How wet you get, like your body is begging to come."

I felt my heart take off in a thunder, growling, "*Hanna.*"

"God, Will. You get so hard." She jerked me, tapping me against her tongue. "You're so perfectly straight and smooth. George would lose his mind."

"I only want *your* mouth."

She looked up at me through sweetly devious eyes. "But I like having you when other people want you. It makes me feel powerful."

"And that's how I know you're secure in my love. You wouldn't have said that a year and a half ago."

She laughed against me, a warm puff of air. "You're wearing my ring. You're tattooed with *my* name. You get hit on all the time and turn into an awkward mess. I've poisoned you for other women."

My hips pushed off the bed, needy. "Don't talk to me about other people right now. I like this wild thing playing with me. I want a dirty little plum sucking my cock."

She dragged her teeth down my shaft. "Yeah?"

"Yeah."

"You like when I talk about how much I love to lick you here? All hard and soft at the same time." She pulled me deep, popping off to tell me, "I want to suck you dry."

"*Fuck.*" Drunk Hanna had a filthy mouth.

"And down here?" She licked down to my balls. "You love to be touched here. I think you're pretty bad, William. I think you like the idea of my tongue all over you here not just because it feels nice but because it *looks* so naughty."

When I groaned in response, she closed her eyes, moving back to take me in her mouth again, deep and up and down, working her lips over me. She'd learned, knew my body so well it was like breathing, being with her like this.

The conversation we needed to have was in the background, waiting.

But it was easy enough to push that worry aside when she was there, warm and wet sliding over me, little growls vibrating down my cock. I told her what I would do to her when she was done there, how I would wreck her with my mouth and teeth, how I would take her tonight and leave her boneless with pleasure.

Desperation clawed like a beast beneath my skin.

It scared me, a little, to not feel like I was getting used to this, to instead feel like I was growing more desperate for her every day. I *had* her. I lived with her. I married her. But my feelings for Hanna were foreign to me in their intensity, and the sheer *unknown* of our future left me feeling unsteady.

Closing my eyes, I gripped her hair, feeling the solid presence of her over me, needing something deeper and larger than anything she could give me tonight.

Four

Hanna

Still half asleep, I winced against the light. It was morning—*barely*—late enough for a hint of brightening sky to start seeping along the edge of the shades, but way, *way* too early to get up.

I threw the blanket over my head, buried my face in the pillow, and squeezed my eyes tight. The streets outside were relatively quiet and Will slept silently beside me, but I could practically *hear* my headache.

Giving up, I rolled over, fingers searching along the sheets for Will and warm skin and—

Oof. That might have been a mistake. I counted to ten, breathing in through my nose while I waited for the room to stop spinning. My stomach was definitely not on board with the change in position.

I groaned, squeezing my eyes closed as I managed to sit up. My mouth felt like cotton and I was probably two seconds from losing everything I drank last night, but this . . . okay . . . vertical was definitely the better choice.

Will mumbled something and rolled onto his side,

and I looked back at him over my shoulder. He was breathing softly, pillow clutched in his arms, sleeping quietly again. His wedding band glinted against the tan of his skin and I reached out, brushing a finger across the cool metal. A week—he'd been wearing that ring for a week, and I was pretty sure I could handle a million more just like this one.

Pushing off the bed, I shuffled to the bathroom.

I used the toilet and washed my hands, brushed my teeth—*thank God*—and drank at least a gallon of water straight from the tap. I never wanted to see tequila again.

Feeling marginally better, I walked back into the room and looked around, my eyes following the trail of discarded clothing that led from the doorway to the bed. Last night had been crazy . . . I thought. I remembered alcohol—*lots* of alcohol—our friends, some vague recollection of Will kissing George and my being totally turned on by it?—I would definitely need to get the scoop on that from sober Sara—and Will's suggestion that I take a teaching job.

And like that, my head cleared. I felt my skin start to prickle as I remembered his comments about me living my life in the lab, as if he was so sure that's what would happen. Why was it okay for *him* to work long hours? To give his career everything he could? Will had always been supportive and proud of all that I'd accomplished . . . Where had this complaint come from? We got married, yes, but I never signed on to be Susie Homemaker or change who

I was. I'd sacrificed my entire life for my career, and I was damn proud of the balance I'd managed to find since meeting and falling in love with and *marrying* him. Did he have so little faith in my ability to handle both?

Annoyed all over again, I walked to the dresser, pulling out clothes and slipping into them as quietly as I could manage. I found my shoes under the bed, and my phone, keys, and ID littered around the apartment and strewn throughout the remnants of last night's debauchery. I slipped them all into the zippered pocket of my jacket, walked back into the room, and shut off his alarm clock.

I was going for a run; Will could stay home.

Just like before that first run with Will more than a year ago—if you can call what I did that day *running*—I paced back and forth, waiting. Over the year we'd adjusted our route, starting at different points to hit the hills at the beginning of the run on some days, the end on others. Instead of the Engineers Gate at Fifth and Ninetieth, I walked back and forth on the edge of the trail near Columbus Circle.

I'm a natural pacer. I did it at home whenever I was stressed about something, and was almost positive I'd worn a path that stretched from the front door of the lab to the opposite wall. When I was little my dad used to say he was going to hook me up to the lawn mower so at least that way he'd get the grass cut, instead of the kitchen rug being trampled to death.

Knowing it was possible he'd already be up with Annabel, I'd texted Max as soon as I left the apartment. Thankfully, he was, and had no problem starting our run a little earlier. Though "little" might have been an understatement.

It was still mostly dark out—especially here, in the park—the sky smoky and plum colored, the edges glowing brighter and brighter as the sun slowly rose behind the trees.

I loved it here this time of morning, when the air was still cool and crisp and there were hardly any people to navigate, nothing to do but shut off my brain and move my body. Will and I had jogged these trails almost every day since that first morning, and were joined by Max and Annabel soon after the little girl was born. He claimed she slept soundly on days when he took her out for a jog, but we all knew better. Max loved these moments with his daughter and Sara loved the baby-free time she got in the morning.

Today, I heard the wheels of the stroller before I saw Max headed toward me.

"Morning, Mrs. Sumner-Bergstrom," he said, stopping in front of me. And despite my current annoyance with Will, my stomach did a little flip at the sound of my married name.

"Morning." My cheeks warmed as I shifted blankets

around and bent to kiss the adorable baby strapped into the elaborate running stroller. "And good morning to you, Miss Anna. How is the prettiest girl in New York? How is she?"

Annabel giggled, reaching for the loose ends of my hair and tugging to bring me closer.

"Well rested," Max said. "Unfortunately, the same cannot be said for the rest of us in the house."

I let out a dramatic gasp. "Did you wake the hungover adult up, sweet baby?" I asked her, pretending to gobble up her little foot.

Max groaned. "Up at the ruddy crack of dawn and then slept the whole way here. Happy as a clam now."

"Well wouldn't you be?" I said, standing. Attempting to make some sense of my hair, I smoothed the tangled strands back with my fingers and used an elastic from around my wrist to secure them on the top of my head. "She's got someone pushing her around Central Park and catering to her every whim. We should all be so lucky."

"I'll agree with you there. Though I imagine William would do the same for you if you asked nicely enough."

"Ha." I looked to the side, out at the seemingly end-less stretch of trees.

"Speaking of . . . where is your Will today?" he asked, following my gaze out into the park.

"Oh . . . he's . . . still sleeping," I said, making a show of dusting off my knees and turning toward the trail. I didn't miss the edge in my voice . . . I'm sure Max didn't, either. Will was still asleep because I wanted a chance to run without fighting the urge to push him into the reservoir. I definitely wouldn't be mentioning that to Max.

"Still asleep," Max repeated, clearly pleased. It didn't take a genius to know that later today he'd be either congratulating Will or giving him epic shit.

"Ready to go?" I asked, and Max nodded, polite enough to ignore my weirdness.

We started at the USS *Maine* statue—Max and Anna at my side—heading down the path that led to the main loop. The trail went from a downward slope to a steady climb up Cat Hill, and I concentrated on the pounding of my feet on the ground, the whir of the stroller's tires on the pavement next to me, all the while preparing for Harlem Hill.

Harlem Hill had always been a good barometer of the kind of day I was having. On a decent morning I could make it to the top and still manage a few curse words along the way—just enough to make Will laugh. If my week had been particularly rough, I'd push on with barely a word, brain empty of all but one thought: *Run yourself into the ground.*

Will knew me well enough to gauge my moods, and apparently so did Max.

"Whoa, whoa. Slow down there, Bolt," he said from just behind me.

I'd been running—flat-out *sprinting* along the trail—and poor Max was struggling to stay next to me.

"Sorry," I mumbled, slowing to a walk and waiting for him to catch up. "I sort of forgot you were here. *And* pushing a stroller. God, I'm an asshole."

Max waved me off and we fell into step beside each other again to cool down. "I may not be in as good of shape as whatshisname, but, Jesus, Hanna, you were running like your arse was on fire. What's wrong?"

"I got a little lost in my head," I said, and it was only once we slowed that I noticed the way my quads were burning, the churning of my stomach. "Ugh, I feel like I'm going to barf."

"Feeling a little rough this morning, I take it?" Max asked, laughing lightly.

I groaned. "You could say that."

"And would this be from the tequila or the husband?"

"Both."

He made a sympathetic sound in the back of his throat.

Anna started to fuss and Max reached down, adjusting her blankets. "Sounds like there's a story there."

"I'm not used to being annoyed with Will. We never fight, so maybe that's why I'm a bit . . . unsettled by it."

"That's understandable," he said, moving off to the side and smiling at another man running past us. "Though if I'm being honest, what I heard last night didn't sound much like a fight to me."

"We get along so well and I'm absolutely *not* used to him being annoyed with me. My brain misfires when there's a hiccup like that."

"Hanna, getting married is huge. Finding a new job is huge. Moving is fucking huge. Doing them all together might make you certifiably insane. Give yourselves a break, right?"

Nodding, I kicked a rock near my shoe. "I know. It's just weird when we don't handle everything easily."

Max shook his head. "I never thought I'd find a couple who fit in such an odd fucking way as Bennett and Chloe . . . but you and Will just might have them beat. Though it is possible you two could be robots. Looking into it, actually."

"Very funny," I said, and slugged him in the shoulder. "I can't believe Will thinks I should take a job without any research component," I added. "Doesn't he know that I love the lab? Doesn't he know it's been my dream my whole life to *run* a lab?"

"Well, he's arse over tits for you, and being in love turns even the smartest man into an idiot. No doubt you all have some scientific jargon to back that up." He glanced over at me and barked out a laugh. "You do, don't you?"

"I mean, there's basic neurochemistry involved in falling in love—or lust, for that matter—and it has definitely been shown to affect brain function . . ." I realized what I was doing and gave him a guilty grin.

"You two really are bloody perfect for each other."

I didn't say anything and instead looked out at the path in front of us. Max was right; Will and I *were* perfect together. At least it felt that way, and I'd never been

Christina Lauren

happier in my entire life than I had in the time we'd been together. But my career was important to me, too, and if *anyone* was going to understand that, I thought it would be him. The lab was important to me. My research was important to me. But so was he.

Why couldn't I have both?

"So how are the interviews going, anyway?" Max asked, snagging my attention back into the conversation. We were nearing Columbus Circle again, and the number of people on the trails and in the park had definitely picked up.

"Good," I told him. "I leave Wednesday for Berkeley."

"Great campus."

"You've been there?"

He nodded. "I have a few clients that live up that way. It's gorgeous, so I try to stay an extra night or two when I can—not so much these days," he added, smiling fondly down at the stroller.

"I've only been a few times on family trips. It could be nice," I said.

"So, not your first choice, then?"

"I don't really have one yet, to be honest." The sound of a siren burst through the air a few blocks away, growing louder as it neared the park before fading off into the distance. Once it quieted, I glanced at Max and shrugged, adding, "Think I'm just trying to get through the interviews first. And trying to imagine where Will might want to live."

64

"Trust me, your husband thinks you hung the fucking stars. You could tell him you'd chosen a school in Antarctica and he'd ask if you were ready to start packing."

"Yeah, I guess so," I said. "I mean, I know he loves me, of course, but the rest . . . picking where we live? It's so huge."

"Well, before all this happened—Will, the wedding—where did you see yourself?"

I blew out a puff of air, watching a small cloud of condensation form in front of my lips. What *did* I want before Will? I'd had a plan—I *always* had a plan—but the days before Will were a little hard to recall. I could see them, but they felt dusty and distorted somehow, dull.

"I never really set my sights on one *particular* school," I told him. "I've always liked Harvard? Caltech, maybe?"

"Back home," he said, and hummed thoughtfully, brows drawn together while he considered it. "Harvard could definitely be interesting. Imagine how often I could remind Will of that time he tried to get a leg over in your parents' house."

I nearly choked at the word *tried*.

Will did more than *try* on that trip, and I basically molested him as soon as we walked into my old bedroom.

My pulse tripped at the memory of later that night. Looking back on that time, I realized Will had essentially professed his love to me, and I had been too thick—or too lost in the amazing sex on the floor—to hear it. My face flashed hot and I quickly changed the subject.

"So it *really* wouldn't be a problem then for Stella & Sumner? Us relocating?"

Max looked at me like I'd just said something absurd. "Things would be a bit more complicated, but you two need to do what's best for you. We'll make the rest work." Then he smiled wide. "Benefit of being the bosses."

―――――

After leaving Max and Annabel at the park, I wasn't quite ready to head home and face Will yet. In fact, I wasn't sure what I would even say to him. Instead, I turned at the corner and headed in the direction of the Fifty-Ninth Street and Columbus Circle station, deciding to take the subway to the lab.

There have only ever been two things that felt easy in my life: one was science; the other was Will. Outside my normal circle, I'd never been very good with people. I had a tendency to overshare, and my verbal filter short-circuited ninety-eight percent of the time. But with Will— somehow—it didn't matter. He found it endearing that I never seemed to shut up, and I never had to be anyone but Hanna with him. It'd always been easy.

But last night . . . I wasn't sure where any of that came from. I knew Will didn't love my unpredictable hours, but that was part of running a lab. I always thought that as a scientist himself, he understood that. Will wanted me to take on a teaching position, but that was some-thing you did when your career was slowing down, not starting out. I wanted to do research and publish papers, contribute to our broader scientific knowledge. I wanted to make a difference. Wasn't the entire beginning of our relationship based on his helping me learn to find balance? I'd done it then, so why was he so quick to doubt me now?

I unlocked the door and stepped into the dark room, the silence immediately pierced by the sound of crunching glass beneath my shoes.

It was just bright enough to see that a shelf near the door had collapsed from where it attached to the wall, its contents spilling out onto the one beneath it and across the floor just below.

"Of course," I muttered, tossing my keys onto the counter and flipping on the light. I regretted it immediately. Glass and papers were strewn across the floor, some smaller shards scattered as far as the other side of the room. And because I was the only one here this early, it looked like president of the cleanup crew would be me.

A supply room just down the hall had a broom and dustpan, and a couple of garbage sacks for everything that would have to be taken out. It took longer than I expected to clean up, reorganize, and stack everything somewhere else, but it felt good to have something mindless to do to clear my head.

With everything done, I put the supplies back in the closet, took a seat at my desk, and powered up my computer. There were a few emails I needed to answer, some last-minute travel details to finalize, and a set of data I needed to check. There was even another interview request, which I filed away until I could look over my schedule and see where I could fit it in. I hadn't yet mentioned this one to Will, and for just a second I hesitated, remembering our conversation from last night.

But it would be fine. I'd get through them all and we could talk about it when we had actual offers to discuss, rather than getting stressed over a bunch of hypothetical variables.

That settled, I went over to the hood to feed some cells and check some cultures, barely registering that I still hadn't eaten breakfast or even had a cup of coffee. When I finally resurfaced again, it was to the sound of my stomach growling through the empty room. It was well past lunchtime, and when I looked around for the first time in what had to have been hours, I realized I was still alone. It took a moment to realize why that was: it was Sunday.

Everyone else had probably spent their morning eating brunch or watching mindless TV snuggled up to someone in their jammies—i.e., not here, trying to squint through a hangover at numbers that could easily be put off until Monday.

Dammit. So maybe Will had a point.

The apartment was quiet when I got home. And—I noted—clear of any leftover party debris. I frowned, feeling like a jerk for leaving the mess for him to clean up, and made a mental note to thank him later.

I let the door close softly behind me and peeked out into the living room. It still looked a lot like it had before Will moved in, bookcases and books everywhere, family photographs on every shelf, and my dad's old desk in the corner. But now Will's books blended with mine: my first real adult couch sat next to his leather chairs in front of the television we'd bought together—our first joint purchase as a couple. The photographs of my family still hung on the wall in the hallway, but his hung right alongside them, soon to be joined by the framed prints from our wedding.

Until we started packing for wherever I moved us, that is, and . . . I could barely bring myself to think about that right now. I'd ignored the growing stack of cardboard boxes that had been delivered and seemed to take up more and more of the spare room every day, but I knew I couldn't avoid them for long. I was nearing the end of my interviews, which meant it was almost time to make a decision, but—*ugh*—I just wanted to be lost in Will for a few hours. To wipe my brain of everything but the way he felt and smelled and sounded . . .

A toilet flushed down the hall, followed by the sound of running water, then the door opening. Footsteps carried along the wooden floors and then Will was there, standing with wide eyes in the doorway.

"You're home," he said, not moving from where he stood.

I placed my keys on the table near the door and slipped out of my shoes. "Yeah, sorry."

"Jesus Christ, Plum," he said, crossing the room and wrapping his arms around me. "Where in the hell have you been?"

I felt myself sink into his body, lost in the familiar, comforting scent of his skin, and hugged him back. "I went running."

"This morning. You went running *this morning*," he said, pulling back just far enough to meet my eyes. "I talked to Max hours ago."

I placed my palms on his chest, feeling the solid shape of it beneath my fingers, the heat of his skin against the fabric. "Then to the lab," I said.

"Why didn't you call? Or answer any of my calls and texts?"

"Oh . . . my phone was in my jacket pocket I guess, probably on silent. I did send you a text saying I'd be gone for a while, though." My eyes dropped to his neck, and I had to resist the urge to close the distance between us again, bury my face there.

He sighed and I watched the way my hands mirrored the movement of his torso. "Hanna," he said, tired.

"I'm sorry, I should have been more considerate."

He nodded.

I ran a palm over his stomach. "I was still upset."

Will pulled away and took a seat on the arm of the couch, and waited. "From last night?"

"Yeah. I didn't like that you just assumed I should take a position at a small teaching school."

"Plum, I didn't assume anything. Is it what I'd *prefer*? Maybe? Believe it or not, I happen to *like* you. I like to spend time with you." He shook his head, laughing a little. "I mean, today is a pretty good example of what I'm talking about."

"I'll admit I shouldn't have left for the entire day, but I told you, I needed to think."

"Well, not to be an asshole and point out the obvious," he said, "but you go to the lab on Sunday all the time. Not just when you need to think. And we were married one week ago."

Oof. Okay, that one sort of hurt. I took a step away, unzipped my jacket, and placed it over a chair. "Going in to the lab is my job."

"I know it's your job, and I love that you take it so seriously and are *so fucking good* at it. But I'm also trying to express that *I* want some of your time, too. And I'd like you to take that into consideration when looking at all this. To talk to me about it."

My head fell back and I looked up at the ceiling. "Are we going to argue about this again?"

I felt his stunned silence before he said, "What we did last night was not *argue*. We can discuss something— even heatedly—without it being an argument. That said,

71

what's wrong with arguing? It doesn't mean we're in a bad place just because we're two people with different opinions about how to handle something."

"If I were a man, would we be having this same discussion? Would a man be asked to take a teaching position over running a large academic lab?"

His eyes went wide with shock. "Yes! You're not seriously saying this has anything to do with you being a woman, are you?"

"No, I mean . . . of course not. I know you wouldn't do that. I just want—I don't want us to argue about something until we know exactly what we're arguing about, or whatever! Discussing!" I said, getting flustered. "We don't even know all the options, so how can we possibly have a logical *discussion* about it? Can we just wait? Please?"

Will sighed, reaching up to push the hair back from his face. He looked at me with soft, patient eyes, and then nodded, holding out his hands to me. "Come here," he said, and I took the few steps toward him.

This was what I needed: the closeness, the certainty I felt when wrapped in his arms. Everything else was up in the air, but this, this was my constant.

"I missed you," he said, holding me to him, palm smoothing my hair. "I don't like waking up without you here, especially with the headache I had this morning." He pulled back and placed a hand on either side of my face, examining me. "God, that had to have been a tough run."

"Max is lucky I didn't hurl on him," I said, turning my head to place a kiss against his palm, and then up, against the back of his ring. "I never want to drink again. I'm pretty terrible at it."

"You are pretty terrible at it," he agreed, watching me. "But you're okay now?"

"Absolutely okay," I said. "Very"—*kiss*—"very"—*kiss*—"okay." He sucked in a small breath when I pressed my lips to his wrist, chastely at first, then wetter, sucking, opening my mouth to feel his pulse against my tongue.

His reaction came in the form of another sharp inhale, and my eyes flickered up to his.

"Yeah?" he said, and I dragged my teeth along his skin, pressed down until his brows lifted a little with the pain. "Right here?"

I nodded, stepping back and lifting my shirt up and over my head. His eyes followed the movement and I watched as his features relaxed, every last bit of tension leaving his face.

"Right here," I said.

We each knew what the other liked. Will liked it to be a little rough sometimes, and I liked to be guided, told where he wanted me and what he wanted me to do.

Will gripped his shirt at the back of his neck and pulled it off, tossing it absently to the couch. "Turn around then," he said, motioning with his finger.

I did what he asked, turning to see his worn leather chair just behind me. I loved that chair, and so did Will.

Loved to curl up in it while I worked, my legs tucked underneath me and my laptop balanced on the arm. I loved when Will sat in this chair and I sat in the other and we were both quiet, no words needed as we read or watched TV. And I especially loved when he would let me climb into his lap, burrow my way into whatever blanket he was using, and watch a movie. And despite having had sex on almost every piece of furniture we owned, we'd never done it there, on one of his favorite possessions—the chair he'd taken with him from home to home throughout his adult years.

I took a step forward. "Like this?" I asked, sinking into the seat, knees pressed to the cushion and facing away from him.

"Just like that." Warm hands unclasped my bra and pulled it from my body. Will's fingers tickled over my ribs before moving to the waistband of my pants, toying with them for a moment before pushing both them and my underwear down my thighs to stop at my knees.

Cool air moved over my skin and I felt bare for him, exposed. I closed my eyes as his fingers tiptoed back up my spine, counting every vertebra, registering every shiver. When he reached my neck, he slipped his hand into my hair, twisting where it was still loosely knotted on top, gripping it, holding it tight and using it for leverage to push me forward, my torso, my stomach, my breasts curved over the cold leather.

"Good," he murmured, and I was aware of him

moving away, of the rustle of fabric as he undressed behind me. I wanted to turn and look, but by the time I'd worked up the courage to do so, the cushion dipped again and he was there, warm along the back of my body. His lips found my shoulder, my cheek. I felt him suck against the skin of my neck, surely leaving a mark. "Love you."

I turned into his kiss and gasped at the juxtaposition of the cool leather on my stomach and breasts and the fiery heat of his body against my back.

Will reached between us and took hold of himself, dragging the head of his cock—warm and slightly wet at the tip—between my legs to brush over my clit. Back and forth, back and forth.

"Want you to open your legs," he said, and I did as instructed. "A little more."

I pushed my knees as far as they would go, flush against the arms of the chair. Satisfied, he placed a soft kiss on my nose.

"You want this?" he asked, stilling just where I needed him, just the head slipping inside before pulling out again. "Want me to play, or just fuck you?"

"Fuck me," I said, rocking my hips to chase the feeling, to get him to move. *"Will."*

"Shhh," he said. "I have you."

He teased me anyway, coating himself in the slickness there before pushing forward.

Will had a tendency to lose himself for a few moments

when he got inside me, to swear or say my name, to whisper incoherencies into my skin, as if he was so overcome to just *be* there that he might come at any second. Today was no exception, and he groaned against my hair, breath coming out in short, hot bursts as he moved slowly, inch by inch until his pelvis was flush against my ass, his flat stomach pressed to the curve of my spine.

"It's so good," he said, teeth nipping at my shoulder, hips moving in slow, grinding circles. "So fucking warm around me." He sucked at my skin and took my breasts in both of his hands, squeezing them, pinching my nipples before sliding one hand down between my legs.

I was wet and slippery and his fingers migrated down, right where I wanted them. *"There."*

"Yeah?" Will asked, and I nodded, whimpering as I felt my body clutch him. I tried to push back, tried to hold him inside me before he pulled out again. We moved together like that, the sound of sex filtering through the room, broken up only by the occasional thump or voices from the people in the neighboring apartments.

He sped up, relentless, and I searched for something to hold on to, some way to anchor myself. I reached behind me, gripping his hip with one hand and draping the other over the back of the chair, my cheek turned to the cool leather. His skin was slick with sweat and I dug my nails in, knowing that would only make it better for him.

Will swore, his breath ragged and hot against my back,

and I begged, not caring if the people upstairs could hear me, the people on the other side of the walls. "Harder. Harder, Will. Please."

"Fuck, Plum." He sped up, frantic, and I could hear the slap of his skin against mine, the sound of the chair as the back legs cleared the edge of the carpet and scraped along the wooden floor.

"Oh God," I gasped, "oh . . . *Oh*—"

I closed my eyes, feeling a wave of heat move from between my legs and across the surface of my skin before everything exploded into sensation. His teeth pressed to my neck, and his hands cupped my breasts, and his wild noises told me he was going to fucking come only seconds before he turned brutal and frantic, pushing so deep into me he was pressed all along the length of my body from thigh to shoulder.

—◦——◦—

We lay naked on the couch, me on my back with Will's head resting on my stomach. "I'm sorry I left this morning," I said, curling my fingers through his hair. "I know you said it was fine, but I wanted to say it again."

He looked up, resting his chin near my hipbone. "I know, Plum. And for the record, you're allowed to be mad and need space."

"I turned off your alarm clock. I wasn't being very nice."

He laughed before leaning over the edge of the couch,

returning with my backpack. "I'm sure we're going to do or say a few not-nice things to each other over the next fifty years. If they're all as nefarious as giving each other a couple extra hours of sleep, we'll be in pretty good shape."

"What are you doing?" I asked, watching him rifle through the front pocket. He lifted a marker before returning the bag to the floor, and pulled off the cap. "Decorating me again?"

He hummed as he began to draw.

A tree, roots that started at the edge of my hipbone and moved down, spreading. He filled it in, eyes narrowed in concentration as the fine tip of the marker moved back and forth, right up to the very edges of the design.

I lifted my head, peering down my body to get a closer look. "It's like yours," I said, motioning to the tree on his bicep, the roots that wrapped around the muscle.

"A little."

"We should really look into getting you some coloring books," I told him, smiling before letting my head rest back against my arm.

"Wouldn't be quite the same, though, would it?"

I pushed my fingers through his hair again, watching the way the colors shifted in the dying light. I could feel the marker move, smell the ink, and when I looked again, I saw that he was carefully drawing individual leaves.

"Now when you go away Wednesday, I'll still be there," he said.

"You're always here," I said, touching the side of his face, tapping it gently so he'd look up at me.

His blue eyes were almost black in this light, so open and honest I wasn't sure I'd be able to walk out the door in the morning, let alone get on a plane and fly to California in three days.

FIVE

Will

Hanna left before the sun was up on Wednesday, bending to kiss my forehead on her way out.

"Bye, baby," she whispered, thinking I was still asleep. "I'll see you Friday."

She turned to leave, but I pushed up, shuffling behind her to the front door, where she had her suitcase and laptop bag packed and ready.

"Can I make you some coffee?" I mumbled, squinting at her. "Put it in a travel mug?"

She laughed when I absently reached down and scratched myself through my boxers. Shaking her head, she told me, "Go back to bed, sleepyhead."

"Think I'll go run."

Stepping forward, she kissed me, and wasn't fast enough to get away before I pulled her closer by her hips, held her tight against me.

Hanna smiled into the kiss, wrapping her arms around my neck. "You're so warm."

"When do you get home on Friday?" I asked against her mouth.

"Mmmm . . . late. Around ten?"

I stepped back, rubbing my eyes. "Wait. Where are you going this trip?"

Laughing again, she stretched to kiss my jaw. "Berkeley." She pecked me one more time and then stepped back. "My cab is outside. I'll call when I get there."

———

"You're being awfully quiet over there."

Jensen's voice pulled me out of my thoughts and I blinked up at him across the table. He was down in the city from Boston, and we had joined Max and Bennett for a late lunch at Le Bernardin.

"Just wondering how things are going for Hanna," I said. "She's giving her job talk right now." I tilted my wrist, looking at my watch, and corrected, "No, she finished about an hour ago." Picking up my phone, I registered that she hadn't even texted to let me know she'd landed safely.

"What did she say?" Bennett asked, misinterpreting my attention to my phone.

"Oh, just . . ." I waved him off, shaking my head. "No updates yet. I'm sure it went great."

"I'm sure they're already begging her to accept an offer," Max said, smiling reassuringly. Out of the three of them, he watched me the most closely today, having heard both Hanna and I occasionally ramble about the job hunt, the idea of moving, the idea of staying, what our lives might look like a few months down the road.

Max certainly didn't want us to move, but he didn't seem all that concerned about it, either. I really could do my job from anywhere, though some cities would be easier than others.

"She doesn't believe me when I say the choice is going to be hers," I told them.

"Well," Jensen said, "where do *you* think she'll end up?"

I shrugged. "I don't actually know."

"And when are you guys planning to move?" Bennett asked.

"Well, we may not be—"

Bennett waved me off. "I mean, when is she hoping to start? Wherever that may be."

"Probably next fall. Though some schools seem to want her to start in the winter term."

"Will," Max said flatly. "The winter term? It's *October*."

I nodded, poking at my plate.

"It's October," he repeated, "and some places want her to start in January, and you don't have a sense of where you might be going?"

"She hasn't visited everywhere yet." The explanation sounded lame even to my own ears, but it's the one she gave me again and again.

My friends nodded as if it all made sense, and thankfully Jensen changed the subject, but I tuned out after a few bits of exchange regarding a merger of two large pharmaceutical companies.

Hanna and I had been so focused on the wedding and then the idea of her career beginning that we hadn't actually discussed the *how*.

Everything felt too hectic, and the *Let's figure it out after the wedding* motto had been an easy way to put off any actual decision making.

Here we were, married, in love, and on the verge of changing nearly everything about our day-to-day lives. And we still had no idea at all how it was going to look.

<hr />

I pulled a beer from the fridge, popping the cap off with a satisfying hiss.

"You're not drinking my cream soda, are you?" Hanna asked on the other end of the line.

"Do you really think I would steal your cream soda?" I volleyed back, settling on the couch. "I may be new to this, but I know how marriage works."

She laughed. "Good. I've been saving it."

"You know," I told her, missing the heat of her body next to me on the couch, "even if you finish it, *you can get another.*"

"Hush. I like the anticipation."

Growling, I said, "I know this about you."

"Will." The single syllable was a quiet plea, a gunshot at the beginning of a race.

I draped my arm across my face, working to not get distracted by phone sex. "Let's play in a minute. Tell me about your day."

She let out a prolonged exhale and then started. "*Wellllll.* Let's see. I think my talk went well. There was a lot of great discussion. And I like the lab space they've suggested."

I waited for more.

Hanna fell silent.

"And?" I prompted. "You like the faculty?"

"They seem great."

Shifting my arm away, I stared up at the ceiling. "Hanna?"

"What?"

"Are you at all excited about this process?"

"Seriously?" she asked incredulously. "I'm *giddy.*"

"It's just not like you to be so tight-lipped about it."

Sighing, she said, "I'm trying to be *contained.*"

"With me?"

I could practically see her helpless shrug. "I'm trying to keep my moment-to-moment opinions in check right now. I figured we would talk about it after we have all the information."

"Yes, you mentioned that, but I'd still prefer to be processing it together as we go," I told her. "I mean, I know you had to take all day Sunday to think, Hanna, but it's not like you really told me much of what you were thinking *about*, other than being annoyed with me. It's a big move." I paused, then added, "For both of us."

"Max reminded me to worry about the job, not the location," she said. "I mean, you can work from anywhere."

I sat up, transitioning quickly from relaxed conversation to irritation. "Oh, *Max* said this?"

"Well, and you did, too," she added quickly. "Early on

you said let's not worry about location, let's just see where things fall."

"Maybe because I expected to be talking about it as we went," I argued, standing to pace the living room. "But every time it comes up, you say, 'Let's wait and see what the choices are.' At this point, Hanna, the choices are every fucking corner of the globe. Can we at least narrow it down a little? Begin to form a plan?"

"I don't know which place has the best offer yet!" she argued, voice tight.

I laughed out an incredulous breath. "Well, we can lay out the landscape so far. I mean, doesn't my opinion factor in at all?"

"Of course, but we don't even have offers from every school."

"Hanna, we can assume everywhere you've been is an option!"

It *sucked* having this conversation over the phone, but I was too wound up to wait. After reading my friends' reactions today, I knew it was absurd that we didn't even have an inkling of where we were going yet. I didn't want to put it off anymore.

I heard her take a calming breath before she said, "I feel like planning right now would be putting the cart bef—"

"Oh, for fuck's sake!" I cut in. "You *are* the fucking cart! You *are* the fucking horse! *You're* leading this. Every school wants you!"

"*Will.*"

I sighed, pinching the bridge of my nose. She sounded so vulnerable, but her placating tone chipped away at my already frayed patience. "What?"

"Don't yell at me. I don't want to fight."

I felt too upset to diffuse this immediately. "At this point, getting off the phone with me or putting this aside doesn't mean we aren't fighting. The fact that you're eight interviews in and I have no idea where you're leaning is already a problem. I want to have it out."

Hanna went quiet on the other end of the line, finally uttering a small "Okay."

Trying to calm down, I said, "Babe, there's nothing wrong with fighting. Sometimes we won't agree. Sometimes we will actively *disagree* about how to handle something. It has to be okay for us to have a fight."

"Well, we just argued this weekend, too. And this one feels big," she said.

"Because it *is*," I answered with an incredulous laugh. "I mean, hey, it's only our future."

She didn't respond. All I could hear was a quiet tapping on the other end: her nervous habit of flicking a pen against her leg.

Leaning against the wall, I said, "Hanna. I need you to say *something*."

"I'm not sure what to say because I don't feel like I can make a decision yet. I haven't been to Caltech. I haven't heard back from Harvard, Berkeley, or Rice yet, either."

"And that's fine," I told her. "All I'm asking is that we *talk* about it, because you *do* have offers from five schools, but you won't even lay out some hypotheticals with me. You loved Harvard. You loved Princeton, but were iffy on a faculty spot at Hopkins and MIT. Right?"

"Right."

And then she said nothing more.

"You only have one more interview," I reminded her evenly. "You've heard back from all but three places. So what are your top three?"

"Based on what?" she asked, clearly getting annoyed. "Location? Resources? Salary? Teaching load? How do *you* want me to weigh these things?"

I let my head fall back against the wall with a soft *thunk*. "Jesus Christ, Hanna. It's like you are pathologically unable to approach this decision. You weigh them *with me*, one bit at a time."

"It's just *complicated*, Will. This isn't a simple process. There are about a million factors at work here."

"Are you really going to patronize me right now?" I growled, pushing off the wall again to pace the apartment. "I know what schools you're visiting when you leave the house, and you generally tell me the specifics of your interview schedule when you get home, but do I get even a single *opinion* afterward? No! So yes, *I* realize it's a complicated process, but *you* don't seem to."

"Maybe I'm just trying to remain open-minded."

"Fuck open-minded!" I yelled. "Be open-minded when you're doing the interview. Inside this marriage, tell me all the tiny gripes and fears and hopes. I don't need the whitewashed version. I want the big and small, the ugly and the awesome. Right now, I know what questions you were asked in your job talks, how big your lab would be, what your start-up funds would be. But I don't have a single clue what you *like*. And you haven't asked me once where I would like to live, what I would like to do. I would follow you anywhere, Hanna. But I want to do so as your *partner*."

She went very quiet, and for a few beats I wondered if she actually had the gall to hang up on me. But then I heard a tiny hiccup and realized she was crying.

"I'm not trying to be selfish," she said. "You know that, right?"

"Of course I do," I told her, softening. "But, look, you have to process this with me, as a unit. Your desire to remain open-minded means that you're not letting yourself fall in love with any one place. And your inability to express a preference—no matter how preliminary—is making it totally fucking impossible for *me* to get engaged in this process." I heard her blow her nose in the background. "And now, your unwillingness to deal with any sort of confrontation is going from naïve to thoughtless. I didn't like the way you used to avoid dealing with things—it nearly ended us before we even began—and I really hate it now."

She sniffed. "I just want to get off the phone."

My heart stuttered. "Hanna. Come on."

"You're making me feel like a child. I'll see you Friday night."

The phone clicked and nothing but silence carried through

the line. She'd hung up. I'd yelled at her, and she'd hung up. Well done, Will.

Guilt and aggravation and just plain dread warred in my chest as I crossed the room before dropping back onto the couch. My beer sat on the coffee table in front of me, still full, condensation forming at the neck of the bottle and running down the glass to pool on the wood underneath. I picked it up and brought it to my lips.

It was going to be a fucking long night.

Jensen jogged beside me on the trail. "Yeah, I'm probably the worst person to talk to about this," he said. "I've dealt with Hanna's head-in-the-sand shit for years."

"No, see," I said, glancing over at him, "this is where you tell me it's normal to get in a fight like this one *week* after a wedding."

This made him laugh dryly, and only then did I realize what I'd said.

I pulled up short, stopping in the middle of the trail. "Jens, I don't mean—"

"You want *me* to tell you what's normal one week after a wedding?" he asked, bending to cup his knees and catch his breath.

"Sorry," I said, shaking my head. "Dude, that was totally inconsiderate. I am a prick."

He waved off my apology with a flick of his hand before straightening. "Given that my wife—previously my girlfriend of nine years—told me one week after *our* wedding that she wasn't sure we were meant to be together, I'd say that you and Hanna are just fine. It's a really stressful time, that's all."

"I guess." I looked past us, down the trail at the line of mothers and jogging strollers headed our way. I hadn't stopped feeling nauseated for hours now.

We stepped off to the side, on the grass, and Jensen pulled a water bottle from that dorky jogging belt of his.

"Hanna has laser focus," he said, and then took a drink. "It's what makes her great at what she does, and shitty at multitasking. I suppose I should give her some credit for consistency."

I couldn't help but laugh.

"She's just trying to be an adult," he said. "Maybe she thinks this is how adults deal with stuff. Sort of stoically."

I groaned, knowing he was right, and marveling at how fucking easy it was for him to come to this conclusion.

"Well, that makes sense, given that she told me I was treating her like a child last night."

Jensen's laugh boomed out in the chilly morning air. "Good luck with that one, Will." He pretended to wipe away a tear. "Holy shit, I don't think seeing you two stumble through marriage will ever get old."

My cell rang on the bedside table, startling me awake. I picked it up, swiping the screen and squinting at the clock: just past three in the morning.

The last time I'd looked at the clock was only fifteen minutes ago.

"Hey, Plum."

"Hey, you."

My body flushed warm with relief. "You okay?" I asked.

She let out a tiny hiccup and squeaked, "Not really." She paused. "Were you asleep? Your voice is all sleepy-deep."

Shaking my head, I said, "I just sort of dozed off a few minutes ago."

She started to apologize but I stopped her. "No, no, I'm glad you called."

"I couldn't sleep, either," she admitted, her voice a little muffled, as if she was lying on her side. "I miss you and I hate that we're fighting."

I fell back against the pillow, rubbing a hand over my face. "I'm sorry. I was a dick earlier."

"You weren't, though . . . You were right."

I nodded behind my hand. I *was* right, and I knew that, but I could have been gentler. Because Hanna was self-possessed in so many ways, it was easy for me to forget that she was only twenty-five and on the cusp of choosing which prestigious university to join, in a faculty role. Talking to Jensen today helped remind me that Hanna had blown through college in three years, graduate school in another three, and then had a post-doctoral fellowship that was only a year—she was still learning how to manage career choices that many of us didn't have to worry about until much later.

"So how was the rest of your day?" I asked my wife.

I settled back into bed as she took a deep breath and launched into a detailed description of her interview: what she was asked during her job talk, the meetings with other faculty members afterward, and, later, dinner with the chair of the department at a small but apparently amazing sushi restaurant in San Francisco.

She talked about what they ate, the mild gossip they shared, and the strange small-world coincidences sprinkled throughout the day, which, frankly, were prevalent in re-search circles.

The entire time she gushed about it, I listened, trying to imagine us there.

I tried to imagine *living* there.

Having grown up in the Pacific Northwest, I could see a transition to the Bay Area. I just wasn't sure I *wanted* to move to California. I liked our seasons. I liked our urban cluster. I didn't want to have to drive everywhere.

I didn't really want to leave the East Coast, and it wasn't until this moment that I knew I felt strongly.

Fuck.

"But, I don't know," she said, rousing me from my thoughts. "I can't imagine us here." She paused and I briefly wondered if I'd accidentally said any of that out loud. "I can't imagine *you* here," she added.

I swallowed, trying to put the right string of words together—one where I wouldn't agree too immediately, wouldn't make her feel she *couldn't* choose a school in California. I'd meant what I said—I *would* follow her anywhere—but there was no denying that a big part of me was suddenly hoping I wouldn't have to follow her *there*.

"You can't?" I asked, hedging.

"No," she said, and it sounded like she rolled over. "You need to be in a *big* city. Bigger than Berkeley."

"You still have a lot of choices in cities," I reminded her.

"I do."

"So, Berkeley is out?" I asked carefully.

She breathed in, finally whispering, "Yeah. I think so. I liked it, but not enough."

We fell silent, and I grew immediately sleepy with the sound of her quiet breaths in my ear. It rocked me from time to time to realize how easily I'd grown dependent on the sounds of her falling asleep next to me.

"I love you so much," she mumbled.

"I love you, too," I told her. "Come home to me."

We fell asleep, neither of us bothering to hang up.

I surreptitiously canceled the car Hanna had scheduled to meet her at the airport and went there myself, on a wild tear deciding to drive the old Subaru from Manhattan to JFK.

The reality of this terrible fucking idea—the traffic, the sheer logistics of parking at the airport—reaffirmed my desire to not have to drive every day.

But when she came down the escalators looking exhausted and sweetly rumpled—fuck it, I would have navigated any cluster of cars to get to her. Surprised, she ran straight into my arms, smelling all warm and sweet and fuckable.

"What are you doing here?" she asked, voice muffled by my jacket.

"I'm stealing you away."

"To home?" she said.

I shook my head. "We're headed upstate for the weekend."

Jerking back to look at me, she asked, "Why?"

Grabbing her bag, I led her outside. "When we got off the phone—*this morning*," I added, laughing, "I couldn't stop thinking about how much I wanted you home so we could talk and relax and get back to baseline. It was this weird antsy thing, and I realized . . . our life is going to change. And I need to know that we can talk about all of this somewhere other than the only place we've lived together. I need to know we can be *us* no matter where we are."

She turned, stretching to kiss me beside the car, and I struggled against the temptation to open the backseat and fuck her in the sketchy parking garage.

The drive upstate was torture, with her hand working my jeans open, playing at jerking me off—but never actually getting down to it. Instead I got teasing fingers, her mouth on my neck, and then the weight of her head on my shoulder as she rested against me, hand warm against my bare stomach as she dozed off.

It was late when we finally arrived at the B&B and

checked in, skipping further conversation and tripping as quietly as we could down the hall to our room.

The room was drafty and smelled of wet cut grass. Outside, crickets chirped and the wind creaked through tree limbs beside the window. It was truly nothing like our apartment in Manhattan. And then Hanna met my eyes, and smiled.

The whole world cracked open.

I pulled her clothes off with shaking hands, tossed her onto the creaky bed. Her mouth curled in a laugh, pale limbs spread across the blankets, beckoning.

The smell of her, the taste of her skin on my lips.

I turned on the lamp to see her better, to watch the flush crawl up her neck when I pressed my face between her breasts, groaning.

The muscles in her stomach jerked under my mouth as I kissed down her body, sucking and tasting her until she was pulling me up by my hair, over her, shoving my clothes off with grabby, impatient hands.

It was fast, and, *fuck*, it was probably a little too rough, but I loved the way her tits moved when I pinned her hands over her head and fucked her as hard and fast as I could.

I wasn't sure what got into me.

A switch had been flipped, some ancient trigger pulled. She'd been gone. I needed to remind her, remind my hands and mouth and cock that *this* was default: us. The setting didn't fucking matter.

She came, but just after I did. I don't know how I managed to actually get her there and not collapse on her. She'd scratched my collarbone when she was close, drawing blood and making me see stars.

I fell over her, heavy, and managed to keep from crushing her with my elbows planted in the mattress near her head.

"Were we loud?" she asked, breathless.

"I don't have enough energy left to care."

She giggled beneath me. "Awkward group breakfast at the B&B."

I rolled off her, dragging my hand across her sweaty torso as I went. "You think I'm letting you out of this room?"

She draped her body over mine, kissing the scratch she'd left on my skin. "Darling husband?"

My blood vibrated at her words. "Hmm?"

"Are we okay?"

Now this—*this* made me laugh.

"Plum." I stretched to kiss her. "Never mind what we just did in this tiny bed, we're *always* okay."

Standing, Hanna walked over to the door and grabbed a notebook from her bag, shuffling back to me.

"Roll over," she said, nudging my shoulder.

I rolled to my stomach and rested my face on my bent arm. The notebook was cool against my back, causing me to startle a little. "What are we doing?"

"I need to make a list of what Caltech needs to bring to the table to beat Harvard."

I turned my head, barely able to see her over my shoulder. I liked seeing that she could admit that, most likely, every school would want her. But I also didn't want her to get brokenhearted if she didn't get an offer from her first choice.

I wondered if I'd pushed too hard for her to rank her preferences, to assume she had her pick.

"When do you expect to hear back from Harvard?"

She grinned, stretching to kiss my cheek. "I heard back from them today."

Six

Hanna

I knew it was wrong to call Will quite so late, but I hadn't been able to call him until now, and I absolutely didn't want to wait until morning. The phone rang only once before he picked up.

"Hey, Plum."

"Hey, you."

"This is becoming sort of a habit," he said, followed by the sounds of the bed creaking.

"I know, we have scripted lines and everything."

"How was your day?" he asked, voice scratchy and deep. We'd been in a good place when I left for Caltech, so I imagined he'd probably been *actually* sleeping, not just trying to. I glanced at the clock and felt even guiltier for calling so late.

"It was pretty great," I said, and noted the pause on the other end of the line. I'd always suspected this particular topic of conversation made Will anxious, but it was only now—since our big blowup—that I knew exactly how anxious, and why.

Looking back, I could admit to having some measure of tunnel vision about my job search. I'd had a list of possible candidates, and I'd checked them off, one by one, not attempting to form any sort of opinion on the outcome until I had all the possible information. I'd been looking at the situation with the logical side of my brain, and quite frankly, the logical side of my brain was an insensitive dick. But now, taking Will's point of view into account, I could see how unfair that had been, and how it was something we needed to do together, as a couple, rather than me telling him what I'd decided.

I'd long suspected that Will would have preferred a school not in California—or anywhere along the West Coast, for that matter—but in usual Will fashion, he was withholding his opinion until I'd had a chance to express mine. Max was right, Will would probably pack up and follow me to Antarctica if I got a job I loved there.

"It was great," he repeated, voice a little too careful. "Well that's . . . that's *great* then, isn't it?"

"Yeah, I mean, they were super accommodating. They must have done their research, too, because they knew my favorite band was in town. They took me to a concert at the Rose Bowl, Will. Floor seats. Who does that?"

He laughed in that slow, sleepy way of his, and I could imagine him rubbing his hand over his face. "My guess is a school that wants you pretty fucking bad, Plum. Did you have fun?"

"It was amazing," I said. "Pasadena is really beautiful."

"It is."

The campus was beautiful, the houses were beautiful, the weather was beautiful, but just like with Berkeley, I couldn't imagine my guy in the middle of it all. Will and palm trees just didn't feel right. I saw him in the shadow of skyscrapers, hailing a cab and maneuvering us both through crowds and traffic while I rambled on about God knows what, oblivious to everything going on around us. He needed little hole-in-the-wall restaurants and adrenaline, a city with history and culture, four seasons, and winters where we could jog through the snow. Where I'd complain about freezing and he'd do something funny to distract me, and we'd see our laughter in the cold air in front of us. And when I thought about it . . . I needed that, too. Pasadena was great, but it wasn't right for *us*.

"It was amazing," I repeated. "But I don't want us to live here, either."

"Okay, so that narrows your choices down to—"

"I think I've decided," I told him. "If you're ready to really have that talk, of course. I know it's late there. Or early? For a scientist I'm really terrible with the math of time zones."

There was more rustling of fabric and I could tell that Will was sitting up. I imagined him naked, sheet riding just at his hips, his skin warm with sleep.

I was so homesick I could barely stand it.

"No, no. I'm definitely ready to talk," he said. "Excited, even."

"Okay," I said, and blew out a breath. I could feel my pulse hammering in my chest, and I knew this was a big moment. "Are you sure you don't want to wait until I get back? So we're face-to—"

"Hanna," he said, laughing. "I'm ready to start the rest of my life with you. Talk to me."

"Right, right. Yes. Like I told you before, I couldn't see you in Berkeley. And I'm definitely sure I couldn't see you in Pasadena. Caltech was great, but not for me. Not for *us*. You okay with that?"

"More than okay, Plum."

"I know there are a few things we're still waiting on, but I think I like Harvard. Their program is amazing; the school is top-notch, obviously. It's a little less money than Princeton, but I think I have some negotiating room there, even though I know New Jersey would definitely be the easiest in terms of living arrangements and the general upheaval of our lives—"

"You know that's not a factor for me," he said. "You haven't spent your entire adult life building a career so you can do what's easiest."

"I know, and thank you for getting that. I see many blow jobs in your future for being such an amazing, understanding husband. I love you."

"I love you, too." He paused. "So . . . Harvard?" he asked, and it was impossible to miss the hopefulness in his voice.

"I think so? They really want me, and I think I'd have

the most flexibility there, which . . . is something I really want. Balance. You remember that, don't you?" I said, smiling into my dark hotel room.

"Balance sounds pretty fucking great. So we're moving back to Boston, then?"

"If you think you could be happy there?"

"I think I could be happy wherever you are," he said, and I was pretty sure he was smiling, too.

⸻

If this Harvard thing didn't pan out, Will and I could definitely not fall back on a career as professional movers.

The first weekend after Caltech, and only three days before our honeymoon, we woke up, made coffee together, went for a run, met friends for brunch, and headed home. It dissolved into chaos from there.

By eleven that morning, we'd accomplished nothing more than covering our living room in folded cardboard boxes. I somehow managed to tape my ponytail to a box, and when Will finally found me, painstakingly trying to remove a strip of boxing tape from my hair, he ended up going down on me on the coffee table.

I wasn't actually sure how it happened.

Not that I was complaining.

In our bedroom, we decided to tackle Will's comic book collection.

The bedside table is where most men would keep porn. Though as I watched Will unload precious issue after issue and then stack them reverently on the bed with a sort of wild, glazed look in his eyes, I realized this was identical to his reaction to porn anyway.

I flopped on the bed and started skimming an issue. In my peripheral vision I sensed Will watching me, brows furrowed and a frown tugging at the corner of his mouth.

"Hanna," he said, gently scooping up a few I might, *maybe*, have accidentally lain on. "Careful, baby. Some of these are older than you are."

"Oh, right. Sorry."

Will began carefully loading them into boxes and I picked up a copy with a particularly busty heroine on the cover.

"Really, Will?" I said, holding it up for him to see. Thanks to a rather large cleavage-displaying cutout, she was practically spilling out of her costume. "I've seen a lot of questionable outfits these girls are made to wear, but this is ridiculous bordering on obscene. How could anyone be expected to fight crime in this?"

"Oh, wow," he said, ignoring my rant entirely and beginning to thumb through the pages. "I haven't seen this in years."

"What on earth is her power? Does she pummel bad guys with her boobs? What is this outfit she's wearing? I think I cover more when I shower."

"This is *Power Girl*, and her costume looks like this for a reason."

"Is the reason so teen boys can wank without actually having to buy porn?"

When he didn't say anything, my eyes widened.

"Oh my God!" I said.

"I think I've got this," he mumbled, continuing to stack comics in boxes with a lot less care than he had a minute ago.

I rolled on the bed, giggling. "Wait until I tell Max you masturbated to a comic book."

"Hanna, *most* guys masturbate to comic books. It's like masturbation training wheels."

"Okay, well, you just made this a lot less fun for me, though I will say your boob fetish makes a hell of a lot more sense now."

And that's how, by half-past noon, we ended up having sex on a stack of old comic books. He might never admit it, but I think Teenage Will just checked something off his bucket list.

At five, Will was going through a box of books in the living room when I passed him on my way to the kitchen.

"Need any help?" he asked, setting down a massive structural biology textbook and nodding toward my box.

"No, this is light. Just underwear, but I realized I want to go through some of it," I said. "Don't have a copy of *Power Girl* tucked in there, do you?"

"She's a comedian," he grumbled, turning on his heel and following me across the room.

"I could leave you alone for a few minutes," I offered generously over my shoulder.

I set the box down on the counter and started going through it. Will stepped up next to me.

"Oh, I remember those," he said when I pulled out a pair of satin panties.

"You do?"

"You had them on at your parents' house when I visited for Easter."

Ah yes, the fateful Easter visit, when no one in my family knew that Will and I were seeing each other. I lured him into my room and convinced him to have unprotected sex while my family was obliviously hanging out downstairs.

Lord. Will's entire life had flashed before his eyes when Jensen knocked on the door.

"You couldn't remember to pick up laundry soap today but you remembered that?" I asked.

"Yeah. Well." Will was quite a bit taller than me, and even standing at my back, he could peer over my shoulder. "May I?" he finally asked, motioning to the box and its contents.

"Knock yourself out," I said, walking to the freezer and returning with a pint of ice cream. Spoon in hand, I hopped up on the counter next to him and popped off the lid.

He pulled out pair after pair, wiggling his eyebrows and kissing me full on the mouth whenever one sparked a particularly happy memory. Turns out, unpacking was way more fun than packing.

"Wait," he said, slowing as he came to the plainer ones toward the bottom. "Why have I never seen any of these before?"

I dipped my spoon into the container and lifted a bite to my mouth. "Because those are my Ladies' Days undies."

His eyes flew to mine. "Your *what*?"

"Menstruation?"

Will nodded, unfazed as he turned back to the box. "Got it."

"You're so progressive sometimes it's actually a little dorky. Cute, but dorky."

He looked back up again, giving me a crooked smile. "You have special underwear for when you're on your period and I'm the dorky one?"

I shrugged. "Well, yeah."

He blinked a few times. "Why do you bother?"

"These days I wouldn't want to ruin my nice ones, but back in grad school I didn't *have* nice ones." I snorted as I took another bite. "*Nobody* saw my underwear then. You know, I even remember a Kickstarter this guy did for something called Period Panties. They all had names like Shark Week or Cunt Dracula. I think there was even a pair that said Rambo: First Blood and had a unicorn that had just been in a bar fight or something." I lifted a bite of fudge brownie to my mouth, only to see Will staring at me. I paused. "What?"

"I can't decide if that's terrifying or absolutely genius."

I nodded, taking the bite and swallowing before saying, "If I'm remembering correctly, it was so you didn't have to ward off unwelcome advances that week. So instead of saying, 'Sorry, baby, it's that time of the month!' you could just throw this gang sign near your vagina and flash your Period Panties."

I made what I'm sure was a crude V motion with my spoon directly at my crotch and then took another bite of ice cream.

"Have you always been this weird?" Will asked.

I stared blankly at him.

He picked up a pair of blue cotton briefs. "What's wrong with these?"

Hopping down from the counter, I grabbed them and tossed them back into the box. "Well, nothing really. Except they look like something my mom would wear."

"Okay, yeah, you've ruined it."

I laughed, throwing a pair at him. "Ruined what? I'm as lazy as they come, and if not for Chloe I'd probably still be wearing the same pair until the elastic gave out. But no guy *actually* finds these sexy."

"You obviously don't understand a thing about men. Or, specifically, *this* man."

I let out a laugh. "I don't?"

"No," he said, reaching for a pair of yellow ones. "I'm

not scared of periods, and you could walk out in *five pairs* of the worst underwear known to man, and I would still want to have sex with you."

"Is that right?"

Will picked up my spoon and the ice cream and took a bite. "Absolutely."

Twenty minutes later, I walked out of our room—naked except for a white tank and *five pairs* of the ugliest Ladies' Days undies I owned—and sat on the couch across from the TV.

Looking up from the box he was taping, Will watched me. "Hiya, Plum."

I crossed my legs, picked up the remote, and turned on the TV. "William."

He straightened, placing the tape gun on top of the bookcase, and walked the box over to a stack by the front door. Crossing back to the couch, he sat on the edge of the coffee table across from me. "What are you doing?"

"Just watching TV."

He looked back at the screen, and then to me again. "But you don't speak Spanish."

I blinked over at him with a glare and changed the channel. "I was reading the subtitles."

Will tilted his head, eyes moving from the tips of my toes back to my face. "You look pretty."

I wasn't really sure what I was doing, and was actually

starting to sweat a little. Why did I always decide to prove a point first and think about it later?

"Thanks," I replied.

His hand curved around my ankle, his thumb brushing up and down along the top of my foot. Moving my foot away, I stood, turning toward the kitchen and trying to remember everything Chloe had told me about being sexy. I think I shook my ass, but it probably looked more like I had a charley horse.

"Do you want a beer—" I started to ask, but didn't make it that far.

Will cracked up, bending over laughing before he tackled me back to the couch. "Are you trying to prove a point here, Plum?"

"*Yes!*" I shouted, trying to escape. "Admit you don't think this is sexy. Admit it!"

"Are you kidding?" he said, tucking his head into my neck and covering me in kiss after kiss. He tickled my stomach and pushed my shirt up to my ribs. "It's been long enough, I could absolutely do it again."

"*Are you serious?*" I screamed, laughing and attempting to twist away from his fingers.

He kissed his way across my chest and down between my breasts, over my shirt. His fingers moved to the waistband of my panties and he slowly tried to peel them down my legs. *Tried* being the operative word because five pairs of underwear don't really fit the same way as one . . .

"What in the actual fuck—" he started to say, tugging at the fabric.

"Just . . . Oh my God, Will—" I curled on my side, laughing so hard I had tears in my eyes. He managed the first pair, holding them up victoriously before he went back for the second.

"Jesus Christ," he said, attempting to pull them down without stretching them or damaging the elastic. "Are these on with some kind of adhesive?"

"No!"

"Okay . . . It's possible this wasn't my best plan. And will you hold still! It's like trying to peel a wiggly onion!"

"I'm going to die of laughter and when the police finally get here I'll still be wearing these hideous underwear. Why didn't you just take them all off at once?"

"You can't expect me to think when all my blood is in my dick!"

"I told you this wasn't sexy. Admit that I was right and I'll just go in and take them off. Admit that I'm smarter than you."

"Oh, you're definitely smarter than I am, and they're *definitely* sexy," he said. "I really don't see a way I lose in this scenario." He lifted my shirt off and over my head and took my breasts in his hands.

"We're never going to be packed at this rate," I said, watching as he took one nipple into his mouth, and then the other.

"I'd say I wished we would have hired someone, but

this has been fun. Today . . ." He kissed my breast again and then looked up at my face. "Today has been pretty great."

"And you're not worried at all about losing this? When we move?"

Will shook his head, placing an elbow on either side of my head and looking down at me. "Absolutely not. It's always fun with you. Remember San Diego for Ben and Chloe's wedding?"

"You mean when we barely left the room?"

Will grinned. "Exactly. You're going to kick ass at Harvard and be the most amazing professor they've ever had. I'm going to figure it out with Max, maybe even open a second office, and we'll make things work. Just like we always do, Plum."

I gripped his hip, pressing into the *H* he had tattooed there, and realized he was right.

This? Was a constant. We could move halfway around the world and nothing would change.

We were going to be just fine.

SEVEN

Will

Max and Jensen patted the table with their hands, a rumbling drum roll.

"How was the honeymoon?" Sara asked, and everyone groaned.

"I don't care about the rudding honeymoon!" Max play-yelled. "I hear enough about their sex life on a normal day. Tell me where you're *moving*."

"I can't take it," Chloe said, gripping the sides of her chair. "I swear to God I am going to lose my shit in a violent way if you're even *thinking* of moving to the West Coast."

"We've decided," Hanna said to the table, "and we are moving to . . ."

She looked over at me, and in unison we proclaimed, "Cambridge!"

A chorus of cheers rang out, with everyone congratulating us both, congratulating Hanna on landing Harvard. We raised our arms in a toast, glasses clinking loudly.

"Boston?" Chloe said when she returned her wineglass to the table. "That's like two hundred miles."

"Are you happy or annoyed?" I asked her. "I can't really tell."

"I'm . . . not sure, either," Chloe admitted, brow furrowed. "I was preparing myself for something really traumatic." She squinted across the table at us. "Boston is sort of an annoying distance. It's too far to drive regularly, but feels silly flying. Plus, it's *Boston*."

"Not to me," I told them. "I'll be down here three days a week."

Sara passed me the baby, searching her purse for something a little quieter for Anna to play with than the spoon she was currently banging against the table. I turned her to face me, puckering my lips for a kiss.

Anna reached forward, grabbing my mouth in her chubby fist.

"Are you staying up there for the holidays?" Sara asked. She returned with a rattling plastic thing before noticing Anna's death grip on my face, which, no surprise, Max was happily witnessing. "Oh, jeez, Will, that must hurt!"

Sara urged her daughter to swap my mouth for the toy, and Annabel promptly used it as a hammer against my forehead.

"Oi!" Max yelped, finally leaning forward to steady her hand. "Ouchie, lovey, be *soft*. That hurts Uncle Will."

"Apparently Anna isn't thrilled about Boston," Bennett said dryly.

"It's okay," I told Sara, leaning in and kissing Anna's cheek. "She should learn these moves. She's one now; you never know when she'll get into a fight in the alley behind the daycare." I kissed her little nose. "And it depends on what Hanna's folks want to do around the holidays," I said. I glanced at Hanna, who just shrugged.

"Chloe and I will host," Bennett interjected. "Dad and Mom are headed to New Zealand for the month, so we'll have it at our place. And I don't want Sara having to do anything strenuous with a one-month old."

We all stared quizzically at Bennett for a beat before deciding in unison to not question his sudden sentimentality.

I eyed Sara's protruding stomach. "You look like a movie prop."

She groaned. "I know. Just get her out of me already."

"When was your due date again?" Hanna asked.

"Yesterday," Sara whined, sweetly. "They say the second one usually comes early. They *lie*."

"You know what usually helps with inducing labor . . ." Chloe sang and Sara glared at her.

"We tried that." She held up her hand, ticking off on her fingers: "We tried sex, and spicy food, and walking. I swear the only thing left is a scalpel."

Max winced bodily beside her and Hanna leaned closer to her other side, putting her arm around Sara's shoulders.

I listened as my wife laid out the details of Harvard's hiring package, and leaned back in the chair, making faces at my goddaughter. Relief coursed through me like a drug and I couldn't help but feel the tightness of emotion rise in my throat. We'd built a life here, and I didn't want to lose these friends. I didn't want to be too far from the people we loved.

We had looked online at houses in the area; we had talked about how our schedules would mesh. We had discussed our shared need to remain near our family: both hers and the chosen one here with us now. In Cambridge, we would be close enough to the Bergstroms that it would be Hanna's turn to hassle Jensen about dating, and close enough to these idiots to share holidays.

I glanced at Hanna as she chatted happily, bubbly as ever. She grabbed a napkin and drew the layout of her lab, before looking guiltily up to me and then flipping over the napkin and drawing the floor plan of the house she thought she liked.

Massachusetts had no idea what was coming for it, but I did.

This beautiful boss across the table from me was about to take over the whole goddamn state.

Acknowledgments

When readers ask for more of certain couples, it's fun for us to try to make it happen. And, more often than not, it feels a little like a family reunion to sit down and write another, small glimpse into their world.

Will and Hanna hold a special place in our hearts because it was the first book we wrote together where we both felt like *authors*, rather than women-in-other-careers who happened to also write books. And we think this grounding resonated with readers in a way that has really endured. So first and foremost, thank you to each and every reader and blogger who has picked up our books, read them, and then told us what you loved, what you didn't love, and what you wanted more of. Without you, there would be no us.

Thank you to the constant MVPs in our world: Holly Root (agent extraordinaire), Adam Wilson (editor with the best margin notes and YouTube links), Kristin Dwyer (our precious, also our publicist—hehe), and everyone in our Gallery family: Jen Bergstrom, Louise Burke, Carolyn Reidy, Liz Psaltis, Diana Velasquez, Theresa Dooley, the amazing sales force (seriously, we want to buy you all dinner and drinks), and each and every person who had to correct our Oxford commas and/or question our "sex-clamations" with a professional tone. You deserve a bonus. There's one for each of you in Adam's office.

We would be a mass of inarticulate garbage without Erin Service and Tonya Irving. Our social media would be a barren landscape without Lauren Suero steering the ship and Heather Carrier making things pretty. Our families keep us smiling, and we keep each other sane, but you, sweet reader, make all of this the best job in the world.

Turn the page for a sneak peek of

Wicked
SEXY LIAR

Book Four in Wild Seasons
from Christina Lauren

"A hypersexy, sophisticated romance that
perfectly captures the hunger, thrill,
and doubt of young, modern love."
—*Kirkus Reviews*

Chapter ONE

*T*HERE ARE A number of things that happen when you haven't had sex in a while: You inadvertently emit a sound during the kissing scenes in romantic movies—a noise that falls somewhere between a snort and an audible eye roll and which almost always elicits a pillow being lobbed at you from the other end of the couch. You can name at least three online adult toy stores from memory, accurately quoting their shipping rates, reliability, and speed. At least two of these stores auto-fill after only a single letter is typed into the URL bar, and you are *always* the roommate expected to replace the batteries on the remote control, hand vacuum, and flashlights.

Which is ridiculous when you think about it because everyone knows the best sex toys are corded or rechargeable. *Amateurs.*

You become good at masturbating, too. Like, *really* good, Olympic sport good. And by that point, having sex with yourself is the only option because how can any man possibly hope to compete with your own hand or a vibrator with 120 volts and seventeen variable speed settings?

The side effects of a less-than-social vagina are particularly noticeable when you're constantly surrounded by three of the most disgustingly happy couples around. My roommate, Lola, and her two best friends, Harlow and Mia, met their significant others in a totally insane, it-never-happens-in-real-life weekend of debauchery in Las Vegas. Mia and Ansel are married and barely come up for air. Harlow and Finn seem to have mastered sex via eye contact. And Lola and her boyfriend, Oliver, are at that stage in a new relationship where touching is constant and sex seems to happen almost spontaneously. Cooking turns into sex. Watching *The Walking Dead*? Obviously arousing. Time for sex. Sometimes they'll just walk in the door, chatting casually, and then stop, look at each other, and here we go again.

TMI alert? Oliver is loud, and I had no idea the c-word was used quite so readily in Australia. It's a good thing I love them both so much.

And Lord, I do. I met Lola in the art program at UCSD, and although we didn't really start hanging out regularly until she moved in as my roommate last summer, I feel like I've known her my entire life.

Hearing her feet dragging down the hall, I smile. She emerges, hair a mess and face still flushed.

"Oliver just left," I tell her around a spoonful of Raisin Bran. He'd stumbled out less than ten minutes ago, sporting a dazed grin and a similar level of dishevelment. "I gave him a high five and a bottle of Gatorade for the road because he *has* to be dehydrated after all that. Seriously, Lola, I'm impressed."

I wouldn't have thought it possible for Lola's cheeks to get any pinker. I would have lost that bet.

"Sorry," she says, offering me a sheepish smile from behind the cupboard door. "You've got to be sick to death of us, but I'm about to leave for L.A. and—"

"You are *not* apologizing because you've got a gorgeous, sweet Australian guy banging you senseless," I tell her, and stand to rinse out my bowl. "I'd give you more shit if you weren't hitting that daily."

"Sometimes it feels like driving all the way to his place takes forever." Lola closes the cupboard door and stares off, contemplating. "That is insane. We are *insane*."

"I tried to convince him to stay," I tell her. "I'm leaving for the day and have work tonight. You two could have had the place to yourselves."

"You're working again tonight?" Lola fills her glass and props a hip against the counter. "You've closed every night this week."

I shrug. "Fred needed someone and the extra hours don't hurt." I dry my bowl and reach to put it away. "Don't you have panels to finish, anyway?"

"I do, but I'd love to hang out . . . You're always at the beach or working a—"

"And *you've* got a fuckhot boyfriend and a blazing

career," I say. Lola is probably the busiest person I know. When she isn't editing her new graphic novel, *Junebug,* or visiting the set for the film adaptation of her first book, *Razor Fish,* she's jetting off to L.A. or New York or wherever the studio and her publisher want her. "I knew you were working today and would probably spend the night with Oliver." Squeezing her shoulder, I add, "Besides, what else is there to do on a beautiful day like this but surf?"

She grins at me over the rim of her cup. "I don't know . . . maybe go out on a date?"

I snort as I shut the cupboard door. "You're cute."

"*London,*" she says, pinning me with a serious expression.

"*Lola,*" I volley back.

"Oliver mentioned he has a friend coming in from home, maybe we could all get together." She looks down, feigning fascination with something on her fingernail. "See a movie or something?"

"No setups," I say. "My darling of darlings, we've had this conversation at least ten times."

Lola smiles sheepishly again and I laugh, turning to walk out of the kitchen. But she's there, hot on my heels.

"You can't fault me for worrying about you a little," she says. "You're alone all the time and—"

I wave a flippant hand. "Alone is not the same as lonely." Because as appealing as the idea of sex with an actual person is, the drama that inevitably comes along with it is not. I've got enough on my social plate trying to keep up with Lola and her tight-knit and ever-expanding group of friends and their significant others. I'm barely past the Learning Their Last Names stage. "Stop channeling Harlow."

Lola frowns as I lean forward to kiss her cheek.

"You don't have to worry about me," I tell her, then check the time. "Gotta go, mid-tide in twenty."

———————————

AFTER A LONG day on the water, I step behind the counter of Fred's—the place nearly everyone lovingly calls "the Regal Beagle" due to the name of its owner, Fred Furley—and tie an apron around my waist.

The tip jar is just over half-full, which means it's been pretty steady, but not so crazy that Fred will have to call in an extra hand. There's a couple talking quietly at one end of the bar, half-empty wineglasses in front of them. They're deep in conversation and barely look up when I step into view; they won't need much. Four older women sit at the other end. Nice clothes, I notice, even nicer handbags. They're laughing and possibly here to celebrate something, which means they'll probably be entertaining and great tippers. I make a mental note to check on them in a few minutes.

Raucous laughter and the sound of cheering draw my attention toward the back, and I spot Fred delivering beers to a group of guys circled around the pool table.

Satisfied he's got them covered, I begin checking inventory.

I've only been at Fred's about a month, but it's a bar like any other and the routine has been easy enough to pick up. It has stained glass lights, warm wood, and round leather booths, and is a lot less seedy than the dance club where I worked my last two years of college. Still, it has its share of creeps, an inevitable drawback to this kind of job. It's not that I'm particularly attractive, or even the best-looking woman in the place, but there's something about seeing a female on this side of the counter that sometimes leads even the most well-intentioned men to forget their manners. With no barback here, I have to do a lot of the running and prep myself, but Fred is a great boss and fun to joke around with. He's also better at spotting the creeps than I am.

Which is why he's dealing with the guys in the back, and I am not.

I'm pretty particular when it comes to setup, and start my shift by arranging everything behind the bar exactly the way I like: ticket spike, knife, peeler, muddler, juice press, Y peeler, channel knife, julep strainer, bar spoons, mixing glass. *Mise en place*—everything in its place.

I'm about to start cutting fruit when a customer leans over the counter and asks for two White Russians, one with ice, one without. I nod, lifting two clean glasses from the rack, when Fred steps behind me.

"Let me know if those kids give you any trouble," he

says, and nods to the pool table group, which is currently whooping about something boy-related in the back.

They seem pretty typical for the UCSD guys who come in here: tall, fit, tan. A few are wearing graphic tees and others wear collared shirts. I study them in tiny flickers of attention as I mix the drinks, taking an educated guess from their height, physique, and tans that they're water polo players.

One of them, with dark hair and a jaw you could probably have sex with, looks up just as I do, and our eyes snag. He's good-looking—though to be fair, they're all pretty good-looking—but there's something about this guy that makes me do a double take and hold his gaze for the space of a breath, not quite ready to let it go. Unfortunately, he's gorgeous in that unattainable, brooding douchebag sort of way.

With that reminder of the past, I immediately disengage.

I turn back to Fred and pull a second glass jar labeled CAR FUND from under the counter and place it in front of him. "I think we both know you don't have to worry about me," I say, and he smiles, shaking his head at the jar as he finishes his pours. "So is it just the two of us tonight?"

"Think so," he says, and slides the beers onto the bar. "There aren't any big games this weekend. Expect it'll be steady, but slow. Maybe we'll have a chance to get through some inventory."

I nod as I finish the drinks and ring them up before washing my hands and checking my station for anything else I'll need. A throat clears behind me and I turn, finding myself now only a foot away from the eyes that were all the way across the room only seconds before.

"What can I get you?" I ask, and it's polite enough, delivered with what I know to be a friendly-but-professional smile. His eyes narrow and even though I don't track them moving down my body in any perceptible way, I get the feeling he's already checked me out, made up his mind, and filed me away in the same way all men categorize women: fuckable, or not. From my experience, there isn't a whole lot of in-between.

"Can I get another round, please?" he says, and motions vaguely over his shoulder. His phone vibrates in his hand and he glances down at it, tapping out a quick message before returning his attention to me.

I pull out a tray. I don't know what they'd ordered since Fred brought them their first round, but I can easily guess.

"Heineken?" I ask.

His eyes narrow in playful insult, and it makes me laugh.

"Okay, *not* Heineken," I say, holding up my hands in apology. "What were you drinking?"

Now that I really look, he's even prettier up close: brown eyes framed with the kind of lashes mascara companies charge a fortune for and dark hair that looks so soft and thick I just know it would feel *amazing* to dig my fingers—

But I assume he knows this, and the confidence I noticed from across the room practically saturates the air. His phone buzzes again, but he gives it only the briefest glance down and silences it. "Why would you assume *Heineken*?" he asks.

I stack a handful of coasters on the tray and shrug again, trying to nip the conversation in the bud. "No reason."

He's not buying it. The corner of his mouth turns up a little and he says, "Come on, Dimples."

At almost the same time, I hear Fred's "God*dammit*" and hold out my hand, ready when he slaps a crisp dollar bill into it. I smugly tuck it into the jar.

The guy follows my movement and blinks back up at me. "'Car Fund'?" he asks, reading the label. "What's that about?"

"It's nothing," I tell him, and then wave to the line of draft beers. "What were you guys drinking?"

"You just made a buck off of something I said and you're not even going to tell me what it was?"

I tuck a loose strand of hair behind my ear and give in when I realize he isn't going to order until I've answered him. "It's just something I hear a lot," I say. In fact, it's probably something I've heard more than my own name. Deep dimples dent each of my cheeks, and I'd be lying if I didn't say they're both my most and least favorite feature.

Couple that with sun-streaked—often wind-blown—hair and a smattering of freckles, and I'm about as Girl Next Door as they come.

"Fred didn't believe it happens as often as I said," I continue, jerking my thumb over my shoulder. "So we made a little bet: a dollar every time someone calls me Dimples, or references said dimples. I'm going to buy a car."

"Next week at this rate," Fred complains from somewhere behind me.

Dudebro's phone chirps again, but this time he doesn't check it, doesn't even look down. Instead, he tucks it into the back pocket of his jeans, glances from Fred to me again, and grins.

And I might actually need a moment.

If I thought this guy was pretty before, it has nothing on the way his entire face changes when he smiles. A light has been switched on behind his eyes, and every trace of arrogance seems to just . . . evaporate. His skin is clear and tan—it practically glows with a warmth that seems to radiate out, coloring his cheeks. The sharpness of his features soften; his eyes crinkle a little at the corners. I know it's just a smile but it's like I can't decide which part I like more: the full lips; white, perfect teeth; or how one side of his mouth lifts just a fraction higher than the other. He makes me want to smile back.

He spins a coaster on the bar top in front of him and continues to grin up at me. "So you're calling me unoriginal," he says.

"I'm not calling you anything," I tell him, matching his grin. "But I appreciate that it seems to be true, because I am raking in the cash."

He considers my cheeks for a moment. "They are pretty great dimples. I can imagine a lot of worse things to be known for. Nobody's calling you Peg Leg or the Bearded Lady."

No way is this guy trying to be cute. "So back to your beer," I say. "Bottle or draft?"

"I want to know why you assumed I'd order Heineken. I think my wounded pride deserves at least that much."

I glance over his shoulder, to where his friends are ostensibly playing pool but currently attempting to hit each other in the balls with their cue sticks, and decide to be honest.

"Typically—and by 'typically,' I really mean 'always'— Heineken drinkers tend to be big with the self-esteem and suck with the modesty. They're also the first person to need the bathroom when the check comes and a third more likely to drive sports cars."

The guy nods, laughing. "I see. And this is a scientific study?"

His laugh is even sweet. It's goofy in the way his shoulders rise just a tiny bit as if he's a *giggler*.

"Rigorous," I tell him. "I performed the clinical trials myself."

I can see him biting back a broader laugh. "Then you'll be comforted to know that I was in fact *not* ordering

Heineken, and was actually going to ask what you had on tap because we just had a round of Stella, and I wanted something more interesting."

Without looking down at the row of draft beers, I list, "Bud, Stone IPA, Pliny the Elder, Guinness, Allagash White, and Green Flash."

"We'll go with the Pliny," he says, and I try to hide how much this surprises me—an occupational necessity. He must know his beers because it's the best choice there. "Six of them, please. I'm Luke, by the way. Luke Sutter."

He holds out his hand and after only a moment of hesitation, I take it.

"Nice to meet you, Luke."

His hand is huge, not too soft . . . and really nice. With long fingers, clean nails, and a strong grip. I pull my own hand back almost immediately and begin pouring his beers.

"And your name is . . ." he asks, the last word stretching into a question.

"That'll be thirty dollars," I tell him instead.

Luke's smile twists a little, amused, and he looks down at his wallet, pulling two twenties out and placing them on top of the bar. He reaches for the first three glasses and nods to me before he turns. "I'll be back to get the rest," he says. And he's gone.

The door opens and a bachelorette party files in. Over the next three hours I make more pink drinks and sexually explicit cocktails than I can count, and whether it's

Luke or one of the other guys who ends up grabbing the rest of their beers, I don't notice. Which is just as well, I remind myself, because if there's one rule I've made that I stick to hard and fast, it's that I don't date guys I meet at work. Ever.

And Luke is . . . well, he's a reflection of every reason rule number one exists in the first place.

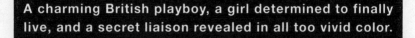
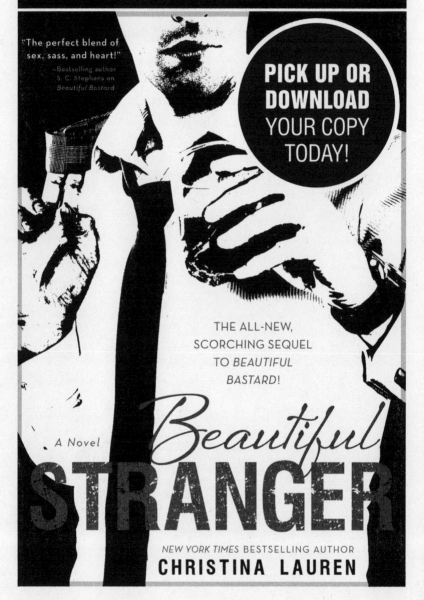

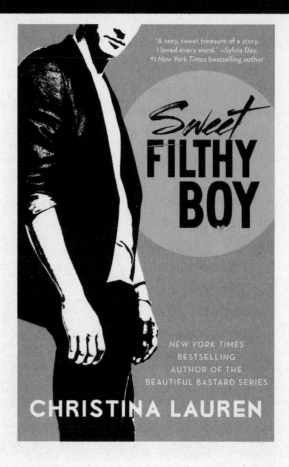